TOMBSTONE SHOWDOWN

This is the story of John Ringo, outlaw extraordinaire. It is a tale of the recklessly brave and amazingly cultured man who drew a gun as other men draw breath and who was profligate with lives, including his own.

Rumour had it that Ringo had been involved in a cattle war in Texas in which his only brother was killed and that his first defiance of law and order had been the shooting of his brother's three slayers. At any rate, his skill with a six-gun, plus his keen wits and his dexterity at cards, provided him with a living.

Other noted outlaws—Curly Bill Brocius and Joe Hill, for example—live again in this story; so do Wyatt Earp and other noted lawmen of the Old West.

As for Tombstone, this is its life story too, for its boom was violent—and short-lived.

TOMBSTONE SHOWDOWN

Leslie Scott

GUNSMOKE

First published in the UK by Wright and Brown

This hardback edition 2008
by BBC Audiobooks Ltd
by arrangement with
Golden West Literary Agency

ISBN 978 1 405 68168 1

All the characters in this book are entirely fictitious and no
reference to any living person is implied

British Library Cataloguing in Publication Data available.

Printed and bound in Great Britain by
Antony Rowe Ltd., Chippenham, Wiltshire

CHAPTER I

He rode out of the red blaze of the sunset to the not inappropriate rumble of distant thunder, the fierce light etching his sternly handsome profile in flame. A tall man, broad of shoulder, deep of chest. His tawny hair, worn long, curled down over the collar of his faded blue shirt. His black eyes, set deep in almost cavernous sockets, were somber, and of a strange brilliance. He had a hawk nose, a long cleft chin and a disdainful mouth. About his sinewy waist were double cartridge belts studded with brass shells. Heavy black guns, their ivory grips carefully checkered to prevent slipping, hung low in cut-out holsters against his thighs. He was smoking a short-stemmed pipe.

Curly Bill Brocius was sitting in a chair in front of Babcock's saloon, a bottle of beer in his left hand, a gun in his right. Between sips he had been taking pot shots at lizards, just to keep his hand in. He observed the approaching horseman with interest.

"That feller," said Curly Bill to Joe Hill, who leaned against the saloon wall nearby, "is too good-lookin' for these diggin's. And smokin' a pipe! I don't approve of pipes."

"Doesn't look like the sort to play tricks with, Bill," the saturnine Hill remarked warningly.

"Hmmm!" said Curly Bill. The gun held carelessly in his lap moved a little. Smoke gushed from the muzzle. The bowl of the horseman's pipe vanished.

The rider's lean face did not move a muscle. He rode on, the stem of the shattered pipe still gripped between his teeth. Six paces from Bill's chair he pulled up, dismounted lithely and strode forward. He paused, spat out the broken stem.

"Mind rolling me a brain tablet, seeing as you've spoiled my pipe?" he said in a deep, musical voice.

Curly Bill's jaw sagged a little. Without speaking, he carefully set the half-empty beer bottle on the ground, fished the makings from his shirt pocket and rolled a cigarette with his left hand. Giving the end a final twist, still wordless, he extended it toward the impassive stranger.

One of the dark hands flashed down and up. A gun cracked, and the cigarette dissolved in a rain of tobacco and shredded paper. Before the torn paper had fluttered to the ground, the ivory-handled gun was back in its holster.

Joe Hill chuckled. Curly Bill still said nothing. He merely produced paper and tobacco again and rolled another cigarette.

"Strike your own match," he said as he handed the brain tablet to the other. "I ain't got but a couple, and I don't want 'em shot out. Matches cost money."

"So do cartridges," said the stranger as he accepted the smoke. "I think we've wasted enough for one day."

"Pull up a chair," said Curly Bill. "Joe, get some more beer."

The stranger sat down as Hill entered the saloon. Curly Bill eyed him slantwise.

"What name you usin' nowadays?" he asked jovially.

"Ringo," said the other. "John Ringo. And it's my own."

"Unusual for this section," commented Bill. "I use two—Brocius and Graham. Don't neither one belong to me."

"I've heard of both," Ringo said.

"What did you hear?" asked Curly Bill.

"Nothing much good, but most of it interesting," said Ringo.

"Hmmm!" said Curly Bill. "And what brings you to Galeyville?"

Ringo accepted a bottle of beer from Joe Hill. He took a drink, wiped his lips with the back of his hand. Then he spoke.

"I decided I'd like to tie up with the orneriest unhung bunch of scoundrels in Arizona, that's all," he said.

Curly Bill's gaze grew speculative as it took Ringo in as if really seeing him for the first time.

"Got any references?" he asked.

"You had one just a moment ago," Ringo replied. "If you care for a more personal one, I can give you that, too, only you won't live long enough to appreciate it."

Curly Bill's eyes narrowed a little. Joe Hill chuckled again.

"Think you're pretty good, eh?" Curly Bill remarked.

"Wrong," said Ringo. "I *know* I'm no good; but I also know my capabilities."

"Hmmm!" said Curly Bill. "Ringo, I think you'll fit into this town."

That was the beginning of a long friendship between the shrewdest and most vicious outlaw Arizona had ever known and the man who was later called the brains of the Brocius gang which was even then in course of formation.

Arizona never learned much about John Ringo. Cultured, educated, splendidly brave, a man meant for better things who had recklessly thrown his life away, he strides somberly across the bloody pages of Tombstone and Cochise County history like Lucifer through the halls of Hell after his fall from Paradise. His antecedents were shrouded in mystery and still largely are. John Ringo was not a man to talk about himself. This much is fairly authentically known:

He was born in Texas and was a second cousin of the notorious Younger brothers of Missouri who rode under the black flag of the bloody Quantrell of Civil War days and later were members of the outlaw band headed by Frank and Jesse James. It was said he had three sisters who lived in California with their grandfather, Colonel Coleman Younger. It was also said that in Texas he was involved in a war between sheep and cattle men in which his only brother was killed. John Ringo hunted down the three men responsible for his brother's slaying and killed all three. A fugitive from the law, he left Texas and drifted west. His keen wits, his skill with a six-gun and his dexterity at cards provided him with a living. He drank to forget, and it is likely that his lawless acts were acts of defiance against the law that he felt had been unjustly used to hurt him. His simple code was "an eye for an eye and a tooth for a tooth," and it is doubtful if Ringo was ever able to understand why the law should look askance at the shooting of his brother's killers. To Ringo it was but an act of common justice, and in his resentment he threw down the gauntlet to all that represented law and order. He was a man of blood who was destined to die in blood, jeering at the law he hated to the last.

His word was absolutely inviolate. To Ringo a promise given was a debt to be paid, and he always paid, to the last farthing.

No man ever discounted his desperate courage, not even the grim and puritanical Wyatt Earp, his deadly enemy, who likewise knew fear only as a word with a rather murky dictionary definition.

An outstanding characteristic was Ringo's almost fanatically chivalrous attitude toward women, all women. A girl from Tombstone's red light district or a lady kneeling before an altar candle received the same courteous consideration and respect from John Ringo. And to show disrespect for any woman in Ringo's presence was an excellent way to reserve a bedroom, four feet down, on Boot Hill.

Curly Bill Brocius, or Graham, as he often referred to himself, was another product of Texas. He was already a name to be dreaded when John Ringo came to Galeyville, but he had not yet welded together the powerful organization that was to rule Cochise County and the surrounding country as ruthlessly as any robber band of medieval times ruled Sherwood Forest. It is logical to assume that Ringo did much to make the infamous outfit what it was. Curly Bill was the field man, the utterly vicious leader when the band was in action. John Ringo was the planner, spinning his dark webs in the background, quietly directing operations with a cold skill impossible to the impetuous Brocius. Without Ringo's intelligence and foresight, ever at his call, Curly Bill would have remained what he was at Ringo's advent on the scene: a minor nuisance who would eventually have been eradicated with little difficulty. But with Ringo as his lieutenant, he was a veritable robber baron with all the outlaws of southern Arizona owing allegiance to him. He could gather a hundred desperate followers within a day if the occasion arose.

Curly Bill's headquarters was Galeyville, the hangout of the real Brocius gang, the compact nucleus of the sprawling outlaw organization.

The Brocius gang! They wrote their names in Arizona history with six-shooters, and the blots and smudges still remain. Volumes have been written about them. Hardly a member who has not received literary treatment, most of it far from factual:

Ferocious Old Man Clanton and his three sons, Billy, who died like a knight of old; lean, deadly Finn; pusillanimous Ike, the one coward amid a galaxy of courage. Joe Hill—his name was not really Hill—the black sheep of one of the best known and most respected of Arizona families. The McLowery brothers, Tom and Frank, doomed to die by the blazing guns of the Earps. Jim Hughes. Sandy King. Indian Charlie, an Indian-Mexican half-breed. Frank Stilwell. And Pete Spence.

There were others, but those were the foremost knights of Curly Bill's infamous Round Table, his Palace Guard, as it were.

And wrapped in the loneliness of his own somber personality, John Ringo, the strategist, the master planner.

Galeyville was named for John Galey, a Pennsylvania oil man who owned the first mine discovered in Turkey Creek Canyon and established a smelter there. The town sat on a stony mesa with the main range of the Chiricahua Mountains towering to the west. Here the mountains open out in an amphitheatre, and through the mouth of the canyon can be seen the San Simon Valley. The main street ran along the edge of the mesa; and all the saloons and stores with the exception of Nick Babcock's saloon, Curly Bill's favorite hangout, faced Turkey Creek bottoms, a tangle of ash and sycamore growth. Babcock's saloon was on the opposite side of the street, which is perhaps why Curly Bill favored it. From his seat in front of the building he could keep an eye on everything that happened.

Galeyville never had more than five hundred people at any time, but more than one individual who went to make up the five hundred was a host unto himself.

Curly Bill had formerly favored Charleston on the banks of the San Pedro River as his capital, but after certain difficulties in Tombstone he decided on Galeyville, farther from the sheriff's office and the domain of the Earps, and almost inaccessible from the Tombstone side.

In Galeyville he held undisputed sway and had already come to regard the town as his own. When he welcomed John Ringo to Galeyville that stormy night, Ringo at once became a solid citizen of Galeyville.

Ringo's baptism of fire as a member of the Brocius gang was to be followed by an exploit that was to cement forever Curly Bill's friendship for the taciturn Knight of the Forty-five who had joined his ranks.

CHAPTER II

Ringo loafed around Galeyville for several days, saying little, listening much. During those apparently idle days he evaluated his companions, individually and collectively, and learned about all there was to learn of their plans and ambitions. He evidently was not satisfied with what he learned. Ringo had no desire to spend his days as a brush-popping widelooper of stray steers or a robber of solitary prospectors and isolated mining camps. Ringo had loftier ambitions. In fact, Ringo was what might be called an "honest" outlaw. In his dealings with men as individuals, he was strictly on the up and up. "Evil's all right, if you get your price," was his code. Otherwise he didn't see any sense in unethical conduct. It was just a waste of time.

During the course of a desultory poker game in Babcock's saloon, the talk got around to rustling, one of the outlaws' most lucrative sources of income. Ringo listened to the discussions for quite a while and took no part in them. Suddenly he spoke.

"Bill," he said, "you're all right, but you're a piker."

Curly Bill bristled. "Piker! Why, just last week

I lifted a hundred head of prime cows over in the San Simon. Got fifteen dollars a head for 'em, too."

"A hundred head!" scoffed Ringo. "And what did you get for them—chicken feed! There's a market for ten times a hundred head every week, and at better than fifteen a head, too. Down there," he waved his hand toward the south and Mexico, "are cows by the million. The *haciendados* own so many cows lots of them can't estimate the number within a hundred thousand head."

Curly Bill looked interested but dubious. "You sort of got something there," he admitted, "but them vaqueros and rurales are a salty lot. They've fought Yaquis and Apaches so long they know all the tricks."

Brocius was right in that. The Mexican cowhands and mounted police had few peers when it came to handling horses and guns.

Ringo did not deign to argue. But Curly Bill understood. The inference was plain. That contemptuous silence said louder than words:

"Oh, well, if you're afraid to take a chance!" Curly Bill didn't like it. He glanced at the wall clock.

"Might as well be tonight as any other time," he remarked. "Joe, go round up Billy and Ike Clanton—they're in town—and Jim Crane and Bill Leonard and Harry Head and Milt Hicks. I think you'll find Alex Arnet, Jack McKenzie and John McGill playin' cards with Bud Snow and

Jack Gauze over at the Alhambra. Bring 'em all along. Tell 'em to sift sand. We got a forty-mile ride ahead of us."

When Curly Bill sent out an order, that order was obeyed without question and without delay. Less than an hour later the band, seventeen strong, was riding south through the late afternoon sunshine.

Old Don Manuel Teran owned so many cattle that when a buyer wanted to purchase five thousand head, Don Manuel asked him what color he preferred!

"I scouted his hacienda just before I rode to Galeyville," Ringo told Brocius. "I learned he aimed to get a big shipping herd ready to move this week, and I learned where he planned to assemble the herd. He won't be looking for trouble, and the chances are there will be only one or two night hawks standing guard on a still night like this one promises to be. We should be able to cut out a thousand head easy."

"Then if we can just run 'em across the Line we'll be all set," replied Curly Bill.

"A pretty big 'if' there, though," remarked Ike Clanton. "We're mighty apt to run into big trouble before we shove 'em home."

"Any trouble we run into can be taken care of," Ringo replied composedly.

His confidence was contagious, and no more doubts were expressed.

The sun had already set when they crossed the

Border and were on the land of Mexico. Two more hours of swift riding through the star-burned dark and they were nearing Teran's holdings. They entered a canyon. The walls at first were long and fairly rugged slopes, but before they reached the south mouth of the gorge it had narrowed, and the brush-grown slopes had given way to perpendicular cliffs of ruddy stone.

In the south mouth Ringo called a halt. "Leave four men here," he told Curly Bill. "If we have trouble, they'll be all set to hold the fort, and to keep anybody from cutting in behind us."

"Good notion," agreed Brocius. "Ike, you and Alex and Bud and McGill handle the chore. And don't go to sleep while you're waiting. Any of you got a bottle on him? If you have, hand it over. Likker don't mix with this sort of business."

Ike Clanton produced a flask and reluctantly surrendered it to Brocius.

"A swig now and then would help keep us awake," he complained.

"You'll stay awake," Curly Bill predicted. "Better not be asleep when I show up back here. If you are, you won't wake up, but you'll stop snorin'."

Three more miles were covered and Ringo slowed the pace. "Right past that grove of cotton-woods is the pasture," he said. "Take it easy through the grove and halt at the far edge. Now if some blasted horse doesn't take a notion to sing a song! Be ready to grab their noses when we reach the edge of the growth."

Pacing their horses slowly, reins taut to prevent bridle irons from jingling, the band rode on. It was very dark under the trees but there was no undergrowth to speak of. They negotiated the grove without incident and peered out from beneath the branches.

The herd had bedded down, fully two thousand head. Only the grunting and rumbling of the contented cattle broke the silence. But less than twenty paces distant, a night hawk sat his horse.

"Now what?" whispered Brocius. "If we shoot that hombre the racket will be heard clean to old Teran's *casa*, wherever that is."

"It's less than a mile from here," Ringo whispered back. "Keep your fingers off your triggers. I'll see what I can make of him."

With which he rode out of the shadow, neither fast nor slow.

The night hawk whirled around at the sound of the thudding hoofs. Ringo was within ten paces of him when his startled challenge rang on the air:

"*Quien es?*"

"*Amigo,*" Ringo answered. He sent his horse forward with a rush. Before the guard could make a move, a gun barrel crashed against his skull. He spun from the saddle to lie motionless, blood pouring from his split scalp. Ringo turned and waved his hand. The outlaws rode from the grove.

Every man of them was a trained cowhand. They got the herd to its feet without causing a stampede, cut out about half the cows and in a matter of minutes had them streaming north. Everything was going like clockwork, or so they thought.

But there had been two more night hawks who had paused together in the shadow on the far side of the herd. They saw what happened. Realizing that they were hopelessly outnumbered, they made no foolhardy attempt to prevent the wide-looping. Instead, they melted back into the deeper shadow and, once they were out of earshot, sent their horses racing to Don Manuel's sprawling ranchhouse, in and around which slept a hundred hardy vaqueros and others of his great household.

Once the alarm was given, action was swift and efficient. One band headed due east at a fast gallop; another took up the trail of the outlaws and the stolen herd.

The wideloopers expected pursuit, but they had hope it would be delayed until the night hawk's relief took over. The herd was still more than two miles from the south mouth of the canyon when Ringo, Brocius and Joe Hill, riding drag, the post of danger on such an expedition, sighted the hard-riding vaqueros speeding across the moonlit range.

The Mexican cowboys knew their business, and they had learned much from the tricky Apaches and Yaquis with whom they were in constant warfare. They did not approach the outlaws in a compact body but fanned out over the prairie, elusive targets in the deceptive moonlight. At the same time they could concentrate their own fire on the drag riders who enjoyed no such advantage. The drag had to keep in the rear of the moving herd to prevent lagging and straying and so were forced to a certain extent to remain bunched up. Ringo realized this and acted accordingly.

"Keep right on the heels of the cows," he told the others. "That should tend to confuse the men somewhat. One moving object looks much like another in this light. Half the time they'll be shooting at cows instead of us."

"They'll be within shooting range before we make the canyon," said Joe Hill.

"Very likely," agreed Ringo, "but there's nothing we can do about it except make it hot for them. Aim at the horses; they're the bigger mark, and a downed horse is just as good as a plugged Mexican. They can't catch us up on foot."

The Mexicans swiftly closed the distance. The flashes of their guns showed golden in the moonlight. Bullets began dropping around the drag riders. Joe Hill cursed viciously as one nicked his arm. Another knocked a steer down, bawling and kicking. Curly Bill's horse barely missed falling over the stricken animal, and the outlaw leader added his profanity to Hill's.

"Hold your fire," cautioned Ringo. "Let them get a little closer."

"If they get much closer we won't be knowing anything about it," growled Hill. "I don't like this."

Ringo waited a few moments longer. "Now!" he said, unlimbering his Winchester. "Rein in, take steady aim and let them have it. I'm shooting at the middle of the line. Bill, you take the left end, Joe the right. Let's go!"

The rifles steadied, cracked almost together. Two horses went down. A man reeled in his saddle, clutching at the horn for support. Another fell sideways and lay still as the Winchesters cracked again and again. The others slackened their pace. A few reined up short. They were getting more than they had bargained for.

"All right!" shouted Ringo, slamming his smoking rifle back in the saddle boot. "After the cows. We should make the canyon before the rascals get their nerve back. Then they'll get a nice little surprise."

The Mexicans had regained their courage and were coming up fast by the time the head of the herd had entered the canyon. Ringo and the others fired as fast as they could pull trigger, but it isn't easy to do accurate shooting from the back of a plunging horse. One man went down but the others came on, yelling and shooting. They were but a scant two hundred yards distant when the harried drag riders sent their horses snorting into the gloom of the canyon.

And now Ringo's wise forethought bore fruit. Holed up behind the rocks with rests for their rifles, Ike Clanton and his three companions opened fire with deadly results. They emptied four saddles in as many seconds and downed two horses an instant later.

In the face of this deadly barrage, the vaqueros wavered. Another man fell, and that was too much. They turned their horses and streaked back the way they had come, the outlaws speeding their retreat with bullets.

"Well, that took care of that!" whooped Clanton as he and his companions mounted and rode up the canyon in the wake of the herd. He was still exulting when they overtook Brocius and Ringo.

"Don't be too sure we're out of this yet," warned the latter. "Those hombres are tricky. Sometimes they skalleyhoot off like that just to fool you. Keep your ears open for hoof beats behind us. Can't see fifty feet in this hole with the moon getting down. If they close in on us in the dark, you won't have so much to crow about."

His warning was heeded and the outlaws were vigilant as they shoved the herd on through the shadowy gorge. Curly Bill dropped back some distance behind the others, straining his ears, peering over his shoulder. He was nearly a hundred yards to the rear when the last of the herd snorted and bellowed out the north mouth of the canyon.

And then disaster struck. The vaqueros who rode east from the Teran ranchhouse had circled the narrow range of hills through which the canyon bored. Now, in the first gray light of morning, they came charging out of the east, their guns blazing.

Taken completely by surprise, the outlaws had a moment of panic. One point man was killed; a swing rider, farther back along the herd, was wounded. Another swing rider had his horse shot from under him and had to scramble up behind a companion. The Mexicans came on, shouting with triumph. The main body was somewhat to the rear of the herd and the drag riders, who were shooting as fast as they could pull trigger.

From behind sounded a dismayed shout. Ringo looked back and saw Curly Bill sprawling on the ground, his horse shot through the head. The vaqueros were racing toward him, making the dust all around him jump with bullets.

Without an instant's hesitation, Ringo jerked his horse around and sped toward where Brocius, who had regained his feet, was reeling about, half stunned. It was close enough for six-gun work, and both of Ringo's long Colts streamed fire and smoke. He emptied three saddles and killed a horse with that withering volley. The others pulled up in confusion, and before they could re-organize, Ringo was beside Curly Bill and trying to haul him onto the horse's back.

Ringo was a powerful man, but the bulky Brocius tipped the scales at well over two hundred and Ringo couldn't quite make it. However, he helped enough to allow the still dazed outlaw chief to scramble up behind him. Whirling his mount, Ringo rode for his life, with the recovered vaqueros thundering in his rear.

But the moment of respite had given the outlaws time to regain their balance. In a solid body they charged to the aid of their beleaguered leader. For those now thoroughly enraged killers the Mexicans were no match. Horses with empty saddles careened off across the prairie. Bodies dotted the ground. The vaqueros who escaped death fled wildly, leaving their wounded behind. The wounded didn't live long.

With the loss of but a single man and four others wounded, none seriously, the outlaws pushed the herd across the Border and to safety. Soon afterward the more than a thousand head were sold to contractors who supplied the San Carlos and other Indian reservations with beef. As Ringo had predicted, the price was considerably more than fifteen dollars a head.

That was the beginning of Curly Bill's robber operations on a scale of wholesale magnificence which increased until his depredations became a subject of discussion in Congress and brought about acrid diplomatic correspondence with Mexico.

For John Ringo did not possess all the brains of the Brocius gang. Curly Bill had brains, too; brains enough to recognize opportunity, and brains enough to listen when an even smarter man suggested something. He listened when Ringo spoke, deferred to his judgment, and when Ringo said a thing should be done in a certain way and at a certain time, Curly Bill did it in accordance with Ringo's advice. And he never forgot that John Ringo had saved his life.

With twenty thousand dollars to be spent, there were riotous times in Galeyville for a while. The loot had been divided share and share alike among the participants in the raid, but a good portion of it ended up in the pockets of John Ringo and Joe Hill, the most expert card players of the bunch.

One time, however, Ringo met his match at gambling. There were shady gentry other than the members of the Brocius gang in Galeyville. Ringo, who was as good at dice as he was at cards, got into a crap game with three such individuals. Very quickly Ringo realized he was being out-smarted, but he couldn't catch anybody at it. Finally, in the course of a pyramid, there was a pot of more than a thousand dollars on the table. Ringo lost.

Before the winner could pick up the stakes, Ringo laid a hand over the heap of gold pieces. With the other hand he drew a gun and let it rest carelessly on the table.

"Gentlemen," he said softly, "I've been thinking. I think a loaded six-gun beats a pair of loaded dice."

A dead silence followed. Nobody seemed inclined to argue the point. Ringo pocketed the money and walked out.

CHAPTER III

Not long afterward, Ringo visited Tombstone in company with Finn Clanton, Joe Hill and the two McLowery brothers. Curly Bill avoided Tombstone, but his followers frequently dropped in.

"Bill knows he ain't liked there," Finn explained to Ringo. "He ain't scairt to go, but he doesn't see any sense in hunting for trouble. A while back he got into a scuffle with the Tombstone town marshal, Fred White. Fred asked for Bill's gun. Bill handed it to him, butt first, but when White grabbed for it, the darn thing went off and wounded White so he died a few hours later. Wyatt Earp, who ain't no liar, no matter what else he is, was there and arrested Bill. He told the court that it happened just that way, and Fred White himself made a dyin' statement under oath that it was so. They let Bill off, of course, but there's been bad blood between him and White's friends and the Earps ever since."

Tombstone was at the height of its dubious glory, perhaps the weirdest mixture of orderly living and explosive violence America had ever known. There were churches, schools, flourishing legitimate business enterprises, community centers, cultural societies, peaceful homes and pious people; but a routine question asked by one citizen of another upon arising was:

"Well, how many have they got on ice this morning?"

Tombstone sat in the heart of cattle country. The cows were there before Ed Schieffelin scratched the hills with his pick and found them to be bursting with silver. So Tombstone, a boom mining town, also quickly became the cowboy capital of southwestern Arizona. The cowhands were not noted for refinement and gentle dispositions. The gentlemen who picked and shoveled and blasted in the mines were somewhat lacking in cultural attributes and peaceful inclinations. The two factions mixed in about the same manner as glycerine and nitric acid; the result: dynamite! To carry the metaphor a bit further, the gamblers, outlaws, plain desperadoes and ladies of the evening added the necessary sulphuric ingredient to achieve the ideal explosive. Tombstone took them all in stride. While a preacher expounded the doctrine of mercy and peace to his congregation, gunfighters died of lead poisoning in the street outside. Tea was served to refined groups at musicales while a drunken orgy was roaring in a dance hall practically next door. Teas and dance hall celebrations were both flourishing institutions.

Early frontier-town drink emporiums usually consisted of a plank laid across a couple of barrels and a pole-and-sod lean-to or a canvas tent. Tombstone saloons were somewhat different. The great mirror-blazing back-bars were pyramided with glittering glassware and bottles of every shape and color. Gentlemen in ties and white coats presided at the "mahogany." And mahogany was no mere figure of speech; it was solid wood polished till it gleamed and reflected. Patrons sipped intricate cocktails cheek by jowl with others who downed slugs of straight whiskey without a chaser. A sober business suit rubbed elbows with a blue flannel shirt, and neither resented the other. When a gentleman began remonstrating with an acquaintance with a six-shooter and said acquaintance explained with another, the proceedings became lively. Peace was generally restored by a bartender or lookout with a persuasive sawed-off shotgun. The bars with their expensive mirrors and fittings were placed in the back of the room, far from the street, due to the fact that exuberant individuals on the sidewalks sometimes practiced marksmanship on the plate-glass windows. It was all good clean fun, but mirrors and imported vintages cost money and it was hard to collect for damage done from a corpse.

Tombstone's hectic activity never stilled for a minute. When a saloon, a dance hall or a gambling den opened, the keys were thrown away. They would not be needed, for the doors were never closed. The blaze of the noonday sun and the bonfire stars of Arizona were one and the same Tombstone. Its growling rumble was as continuous as the thunder of the stamp mills at Charleston and Contention grinding out the silver that was Tombstone's life blood. The great ore wagons drawn by sixteen mules constantly rumbled through the town, bearing to the mills the product of Contention, the Lucky Cuss, the Sulphuret, the Goodenough, the East Side, and West Side, the Tough Nut and the other great mines. After the mighty stamps did their ponderous dance, pulverizing the ore to a watery paste, and the precious metal was extracted by the amalgam process, the silver bullion was cast in two-hundred-pound bars which gentlemen of easy morals and acquisitive dispositions found difficult to transport via horseback. Which went far toward insuring that the metal would reach its proper destination and not end up in the dubious company of certain citizens of Galeyville.

More than $80,000,000 worth of minerals were taken from the Tombstone mines during the brief period of their existence.

Tombstone's principal thoroughfare was Allen Street, paralleled by Tough Nut and Fremont. All three were business centers. Allen was wide, lined with business houses from the O.K. corral at one end to the Bird Cage Opera House, bawdy and notorious, at the other. Wall Street, New York, ends in a graveyard. Allen Street also ended at a place of death, for it was in the O.K. corral that the famous gunfight between the Earp faction and members of Curly Bill's gang occurred.

A unique feature of Allen Street was its wooden awnings—projecting roofs that were supported by posts at the curbs—that warded off rain and the fierce rays of the Arizona sun. Crowds swarmed continuously, day and night, under these long, sheltering arcades.

On Allen Street, at the corner of Fourth, was the Can-Can Restaurant, famed for its delicacies. It employed hunters to provide it with bear, deer and antelope, and imported lobsters and fish from Guaymas, Mexico, by fast stage.

At the northwest corner of Allen and Fifth was the Crystal Palace Saloon, one of the most luxurious and famous of Tombstone's saloons and gambling houses. It had well-designed French windows, doors and trim. Splendid paintings hung on the walls, the bar was of finest mahogany and was presided over by from three to five bartenders. The gambling tables were always crowded and the play was steep. During the late hours of the night, the Crystal Palace was the favorite haunt of women from the shadier resorts and their questionable companions. The place was always packed during these hours, and the drinking, gambling and general rambunctious celebrating roared on until long past daylight.

Across from the Crystal Palace, on the northeast corner of Allen and Fifth, was the equally famous Oriental Bar in which Wyatt Earp owned an interest. This was the hangout of the Earp faction. Wyatt, Virgil and Morgan Earp could usually be found there, in company with gaunt, consumptive Doc Holliday, the Earps' trigger man, with Buckskin Frank Leslie, said by many to be the deadliest gunslinger the West ever knew, presiding as head bartender and looking genial and harmless in his white garb. . . .

Ringo and his companions stabled their horses and proceeded to do the town. They fortified themselves with drinks in some of the rougher saloons in the region of red lights and murky dance halls adjoining the business district. Then they gravitated to Allen Street.

"This looks like a good one," remarked Ringo, pausing in front of the open doors of the Oriental Bar.

"We don't go in there," replied Finn Clanton.

"Why not?" Ringo asked.

"That's Wyatt Earp's place," Finn explained. "There are always Earp men in there. No sense in looking for trouble. Come on; we'll go across the street to the Crystal Palace. Sheriff Behan and his bunch will be there, and they're our friends."

"Think I'll drop in here," said Ringo, and suited the action to the word.

The Oriental was strangely quiet as Ringo

walked to the bar, which was some twenty feet back from the door and windows, as a safety measure. Wyatt Earp, tall, blond, cold-eyed and poker-faced, stood at the far end of the bar with his soldierly-looking elder brother, Virgil, town marshal of Tombstone, and saturnine, cadaverous Doc Holliday impeccably garbed in gray but with the set of his coat slightly spoiled by the sawed-off shotgun strapped under his left arm. Buckskin Frank was behind the bar.

The genial Leslie served Ringo with a smile and a nod, but in silence. The group at the end of the bar regarded him gravely.

Wyatt left his place and walked up to Ringo, who turned to face him. Wyatt was a tall man, but he had to raise his eyes slightly to meet Ringo's glittering black gaze.

"New man around here?" Wyatt asked in his deep voice.

"A misuse of the English language, but I suppose it states the case," Ringo replied.

Wyatt seemed a trifle taken aback at the answer he got. He looked Ringo over with increased interest.

"Saw you were in rather bad company out there," he remarked, jerking his head toward the street where Ringo had paused with his companions, who had discreetly repaired to the Crystal Palace.

"My company is of my own choosing," Ringo said.

The reply and the cold voice in which it was spoken irritated the marshal.

"Where'd you come from?" he asked abruptly. "I don't ask you where you came from," Ringo answered. "And I don't think you have any more right to ask me such a question than I have to ask it of you. If you're speaking as a peace officer, you're talking out of turn and you know it. If you're speaking as an individual, you can get any kind of an answer you're looking for."

Wyatt Earp, a fair man, considered that. "Guess you're right," he said. "No offense meant."

"None taken," Ringo said.

Wyatt walked back to his companions. Ringo had another drink and left.

"Wyatt," said Virgil Earp, gazing after Ringo's broad back, "that is a dangerous man. Who is he?"

"I don't know," Wyatt answered, "but I intend to find out."

He did find out, and John Ringo from there on proved to be a thorn in the marshal's side in more ways than one.

Ringo left the Oriental in a black and bitter mood. He had meant it when he said he had not taken offense, but nevertheless he felt that he had been done an injustice. Wyatt had intimated plainly that he was not a desirable character to have around, doubtless because of his evident intimacy with Clanton, Joe Hill and the McLowery brothers. The seeds of hate had been sown, and the resultant growth would bear bitter fruit.

When Ringo entered the Crystal Palace, one glance at his face made his companions decide not to ask questions. They felt it would be unwise, to say the least. In fact, hard men though they were, his associates were already a little afraid of John Ringo. They had no desire to rouse the devil that always lay ready and waiting behind his impassive countenance and somber eyes.

Ringo was introduced to bustling, voluble Sheriff Behan, who was having a drink with the boys. Strange to say, Ringo took a liking to the pompous little man. Perhaps his discerning eye saw the real worth of Johnny Behan that did not show on the surface. John Behan was in many ways a small-calibre man, but a shrewder politician never settled in Tombstone. He was a natural gladhander, an oily manipulator with a genius for making better men do his bidding. His first and only term as a peace officer was tumultuous, as might have been expected, and after he was indicted by a grand jury for acts perpetrated while in office, Johnny left Tombstone about two jumps ahead of his successor. But he was a good friend to his friends, and he did not lack courage.

Ringo also met Billy Breckenridge, Behan's deputy, a smiling, handsome young fellow whose friendly eyes and debonair manner masked dauntless courage and a cold, calculating brain that made few mistakes. A man who brushed shoulders with outlaws and scheming politicians in the course of his long and eventful career and was able to keep his hands clean and his record spotless. He spent his last days, when well up in his eighties or perhaps a little older, at the Old Pueblo Club or at the Arizona Pioneers Historical Society in Tucson. Ringo liked Breckenridge and was to meet with him frequently, both socially and officially.

"Johnny Behan's all right, and so is Billy," Finn Clanton remarked as they prepared to leave town the following afternoon, their pockets light but their faces ashine with pleasant memories. "Johnny's a shrewd number," he added. "The Earps are salty, but I'm bettin' on Johnny to come out on top when they have the final showdown as to who's to run this town."

"Very likely you're right," Ringo agreed. "Guts and a quick trigger finger aren't enough to get you on top. Brains win out in the end."

CHAPTER IV

Ringo was riding alone a great deal. He liked to be by himself but his riding was not altogether pastime. Money was running a bit low in Galeyville and something had to be done. Curly Bill suggested another raid into Mexico for more cattle, but Ringo had an idea knocking about in his mind and he told Brocius to hold up a bit.

The caravans constantly coming up from Mexico interested Ringo. He knew that the majority of them were smuggling trains and that often the great rawhide aparejos—packsaddles that half hid the small, lithe Andalusian mules, were bulging with silver 'dobe dollars that would be exchanged in Tucson or some other place for goods that would never be fingered by the Customs agents; goods that would bring a huge profit in the interior of Mexico. Sitting his horse at some spot where he could see and not be seen, Ringo speculated on those packsaddles that fitted snugly around the curving side of the mules and were strapped securely beneath their bellies. Ringo did not covet the aparejos, but their contents, those opulent 'dobe dollars, were something else again.

The question was, how to get them? The msuggling routes were carefully chosen to minimize the danger of an ambush. The trains were always heavily guarded by armed outriders who paced their horses before, behind and along the line of mules, on either side. And those dark-faced men from below the Line were grim and efficient fighters.

One particular train that appeared with clockwork regularity quickened Ringo's interest. It was always large, always headed by the same man, a tall, handsome, finely set-up Mexican whose steeple sombrero was ornamented with silver bangles, whose buckskin pantaloons had pearl buttons, and who wore his striped resplendent *serape* swathed across his chest and shoulders in the graceful sweeping fashion affected by the hidalgos. Ringo did not think he was truly a nobleman, but he had the bearing and the manner.

One day when the train appeared, Ringo followed it at a discreet distance. He followed it to Tucson and, keeping well under cover, learned all he could about it and its courtly leader. He learned that the man was Miguel Garcia who claimed to be a Don but very likely wasn't. Ringo learned that he stood well with the "authorities" and had the reputation of being an honest smuggler who respected the law so long as it did not interfere with his lucrative business. He paid tribute with a generous hand and was meticulously fair in his dealings. The merchants of Tucson liked to deal with Miguel Garcia. He bought heavily, paid what was asked, and always came back for more. The respectable merchants doubtless reflected that what he did with the goods after he removed them from the stores and warehouses was no concern of theirs. Ringo had no difficulty learning when Garcia was expected to arrive again in Tucson with his bulging aparejos.

After leaving Tucson, Ringo rode the smuggler trail from the Border northward. He finally decided that his best bet was Skeleton Canyon, through which the train coming up from Mexico by way of San Luis Pass through the Animas Mountains and across the Animas Valley would have to pass.

Yes, Skeleton Canyon was the best bet, but it was none too good. There was little cover that could be trusted. Near where it opened out into the San Simon Valley the canyon was brush-grown, but the brush thinned out as it approached the trail. Men holed up in that thin brush would most certainly be spotted by the hawk-eyed smugglers. Ringo had no desire to fight a pitched battle with the dark riders. That would be altogether too high a price to pay for the contents of the aparejos.

Sitting his horse in the canyon mouth, Ringo formed a plan; a daring plan fraught with great personal danger, but one he believed would work. That it involved mass murder bothered him no more than did the risk he would be taking. His was the attitude of the old-time Texan, best illustrated by a remark made by Jerry Barton, noted for his strength and ferocity and said to have killed seventeen men, three in handkerchief duels and two with his fists. Somebody asked Jerry how many people he had killed in the course of his turbulent career. Jerry thought awhile and then asked, "Do Mexicans count?"

When Ringo returned to Galeyville and unfolded his plan, his hearers stared at him speechless for a moment. Finally Joe Hill spoke.

"John," he asked, "are you plumb tired of living? You'll be dead in ten seconds after you try to go through with that fool scheme."

"I'll take the chance," Ringo replied composedly. "And I don't figure to die unless you fellows bungle your end."

To which Curly Bill answered, "If we do, the chances are we'll all be cashed in. Those smugglers are tough hombres, and when they shoot they don't miss. But you call the play and we'll follow your lead."

Miguel Garcia was in a jovial mood as he rode at the head of his long mule train. His black eyes gleamed with anticipation as he envisioned the pleasures to be had at Tucson after the merchants had come to his camp outside the town and the trading was finished. He had been working hard, and felt that he and his men were entitled to a bit of diversion. He hummed a little tune and tickled his mettlesome horse with his spurs, causing the animal to prance and cavort and his alertly vigilant outriders to chuckle. But while they spared a glance now and then for their debonair leader, their sharp eyes were constantly probing the brush, the more distant groves and any other nook that might conceal an enemy.

Garcia's cheerfulness increased as they neared the canyon mouth. Ahead was the broad valley and easy going to Tucson. The worst part of the trip was just about over.

The caravan swung around a bend. Instantly the vigilance increased four-fold. Sitting his horse in the middle of the trail was a tall man with yellow hair hanging down over his coat collar. A rifle rested across his saddlebow; heavy six-guns sagged against his thighs. On his broad breast gleamed the silver shield of a deputy United States marshal. He held up his hand imperatively.

"Hold it!" he shouted.

Instantly twenty guns were trained on the lone horseman. The caravan jingled to a halt.

"Put up those guns!" Ringo called. "I don't think you fellows are going in for killing peace officers just yet. Garcia, we don't mind looking the other way a bit when you stick to honest smuggling—we know you always pay your dues

—but this business of slipping Chinese into Arizona has got to stop. We don't want them here."

"*Señor!*" gasped the scandalized Garcia. "*Señor*, I never did such a thing in my life!"

"No?" The "marshal" was plainly skeptical. "No? Well, I've heard that you're running 'em in, disguised as outriders. I want to give every one of your men a close once-over."

"*Señor*, look!" replied Garcia. "Look closely as you will. If you find a man of China among my men I will give you his weight in silver."

"I'll hold you to that," the other warned as he shoved his rifle into the saddle boot and rode slowly forward to peer into grinning faces with the carping gaze of one who is not likely to be easily convinced.

From man to man he rode. One dark little fellow at the rear end of the line, who undoubtedly had a preponderance of Indian blood, seemed to excite his suspicion. He reined in, his eyes hard on the other's face.

"Open your shirt!" he ordered.

Chuckling, the man obeyed, displaying a hairy chest as dark as his face. Ringo wagged his head disgustedly.

"Garcia, looks like you got a clean slate this time, anyhow," he called. "Okay, have a good time at Tucson, but watch your step. You're liable to meet me when you least expect to."

"It will always be the pleasure, *señor*," the Mexican courteously replied.

Thrown off balance by the amazing accusation, absorbed in the doings of the supposed marshal, neither Garcia nor his men saw the silent figures stealing through the sparse brush on either side of the trail. A roar of gunfire was the first intimation that danger was near. That storm-blast of death emptied saddles right and left. Miguel Garcia was the first to fall. Curly Bill, ferocious Old Man Clanton and the others ran forward, shooting as they ran. Ringo had jerked his guns and was killing the rear guard.

The smugglers tried to fight back, but they never had a chance. Demoralized by the death of their leader, caught between a deadly crossfire, they died. Only one escaped, a young fellow, little more than a boy. Wounded, mad with terror, he spurred his frantic horse past Ringo and vanished down the canyon. Ringo could have killed him, but let him go. That act of mercy was destined to thin out the Brocius gang. The Mexican had recognized certain faces, including particularly the bearded visage of Old Man Clanton.

Nineteen Mexicans died in the bloody affair. Those who took part in the raid, beside Brocius and Ringo, were, it is said, Old Man Clanton, his sons, Ike and Billy, Joe Hill, the McLowery brothers, Tom and Frank, Charlie Snow and several others. The killers suffered no casualties.

From the aparejos were taken more than $75,000 in Mexican silver. Galeyville, Charleston, Paradise and Tombstone saw a spending spree that was something to remember.

The exploit established Ringo firmly as the real leader of the gang. Curly Bill deferred to him and followed any suggestion he made. The others took no chances with his formidable temper and the uncertainties of his dark mind.

But Ringo never assumed an active leadership. His interest in his associates, their doings and their fates was not strong enough. To him they were but a means to an end, shadows among whom he walked a darker shadow. He drank heavily, gambled most of the time and spoke rarely. Unlike the others, who seldom visited the silver town, he rode frequently to Tombstone. He would stalk Indian-like into the Oriental Bar, filled with Earp men, and drink with Buckskin Frank Leslie, who always served him. The Earps let him severely alone. If he made trouble they could take care of it, but they had no intention of starting trouble with Ringo.

Only Doc Holliday, a born killer, eyed Ringo hopefully. "I have the advantage, even with Ringo," the cadaverous dentist was wont to say. "I'm so thin nobody can hit me!"

He believed it. And what was more, he proved it. He died in bed, of consumption.

Ringo never forgave Wyatt Earp for his initial greeting. The thing rankled in his mind, especially when he had been drinking. One day he decided on a showdown. He met Wyatt Earp and Doc Holliday in front of the saloon.

"Wyatt," he said, "you and your bunch hate me and my bunch. Sooner or later, there's going to be trouble. I've figured a good way to settle the whole business and keep others out of it. You and I will pace off ten steps, turn, and shoot it out. What say?"

Wyatt Earp gazed at Ringo. There was no fear in his eyes, only calculation.

"Ringo," he answered, "it isn't a fair proposition. It's even money I'll kill you and you'll kill me."

"Then why isn't it fair?" Ringo asked.

"Because," Wyatt replied slowly, "I have no desire to die just yet, while you don't give a hoot. You figure it's a nice way to satisfy a grudge and commit suicide at the same time. You'll do that last in the end, anyhow. I don't intend to give you the satisfaction of doing it for you."

Ringo was somewhat taken aback. As fair a man in his own peculiar way as Earp himself, he had to admit that Wyatt had stated the case precisely.

Doc Holliday looked hopeful. "Wyatt, I've a notion to take John up on it," he said.

"No, you won't," Wyatt returned. "The result would be the same as if I took him up, and I've got use for you for a while yet."

He took Holliday by the arm and led him into the saloon.

Baffled, Ringo crossed the street to the Crystal Palace and proceeded to get drunk with Johnny Behan.

CHAPTER V

Differing from his associates, who seldom troubled themselves with much beyond the facts of life and the ways of Mexicans, Ringo's nature was complex. He did not fit readily into the accepted pattern of an outlaw. He was never coarse or vulgar. His speech was not the rough language of the frontier. Never, not even in moments of the greatest stress, did John Ringo forget that he had been born and reared a gentleman. Drink merely served to accentuate his cultural carriage and poise. Even when he killed a man, John Ringo did so courteously.

Ringo was violently opposed to bad manners and to bad language in any form. His objection sometimes manifested itself in a grim and grisly manner. A gentleman by the name of Withrow, Buck Withrow he called himself, who claimed to be from the Pecos country, offended Ringo's sensibilities in the Crystal Palace Saloon. Ringo knocked him cold with one blow of his fist. Later, when he recovered his senses, Withrow vowed vengeance. His opportunity came the next day in the streets of Charleston. Withrow, mounted and brandishing a double-barrelled shotgun, came charging down the street toward where Ringo stood. He was howling threats and obscenities.

Withrow's choice of weapons was bad. The range of a shotgun is limited. It is much less than that of a Colt Forty-five. Ringo watched him come, coolly rolling a cigarette with his left hand the while. He estimated the distance to a nicety. When Withrow was just outside accurate, shotgun range, Ringo drew his gun and, something unusual for him, took careful and deliberate aim. He shot Withrow through the mouth.

"I didn't like the way he talked," Ringo explained as he regarded the corpse of his adversary. "I figured he needed his mouth washed out."

Ringo was even known to turn his hand, when the fancy struck him, to legitimate enterprise. The Crawford cattle drive was an example.

Old Sam Crawford was an honest rancher who had grown weary of the continual strife and bloodshed in the Animas Valley. While he had little formal education, he was widely read and a good conversationalist. Ringo used to drop in at the Rafter S for a cup of coffee and a gab. One day while they sat on the front porch gazing toward the dark mouth of Skeleton Canyon, Crawford remarked:

"John, if I could tie onto a good trail boss who knows the country between here and there, I'd pull up stakes and move over to California. My brother, who owned a spread over there, beyond the Mojave, died recently, and I guess the holdings are mine now. His range boss is handling things at present, and he writes me it's a good holding, with plenty of water, a nice climate and that the markets ain't bad. I'm plumb tired of the ructions in this section. Got so a man can't enjoy a minute's peace of mind for wondering what's going to bust loose next."

Ringo looked contemplative. "Other side of the Mojave?" he inquired.

"That's right," replied Crawford.

"Be a hard drive across the desert, but it can be done by a man who knows the country," Ringo said. "You really mean it, Sam?"

"I sure do," declared Crawford. "That is, if I had a man who could handle the drive. I can't trust any of my boys. They're good hands, but they ain't got sense enough to pour water out of a boot with directions writ on the heel. And I'm a mite too old and stove up to handle such a chore. Yes, if I could get a man, I'd sure pull up stakes pronto."

Ringo gazed toward Skeleton Canyon. Perhaps he was thinking of what had happened there not so long before. Perhaps he was suffering a little remorse in a sober moment. Or perhaps he was moved by some other emotion that at the moment controlled his somber mind. He turned toward Crawford.

"Sam," he said, "I'm your huckleberry."

Crawford stared. "You really mean it?"

"I do," Ringo answered. "I know the country.

Fact is, I came here across the Mojave. Had been fooling around over west of there. Had a notion I'd like to visit my sisters who live in California. Came nigh to doing it, but changed my mind at the last minute. Figured I'd do better to stay away. They think I'm an honest cattleman here in Arizona. An honest cattleman! Best to let them keep on thinking it. If they got a look at me now, the chances are they'd know different. Yes, I'll go along with you, Sam. Do me good to get away from this section for a spell."

Crawford, who was itching to get away from Arizona, jumped at the chance. So the next morning saw the grim outlaw superintending the prosaic business of rounding up a trail herd and getting it ready for the drive.

The work proceeded apace, for when Ringo gave an order it was obeyed instantly and without question. The Rafter S hands felt that to do otherwise would be detrimental to their health and well-being.

The word got around, of course. Some people were plainly suspicious.

"Crawford will lose his herd before it is out of sight of the *casa*," these skeptics declared. "Ringo has got something up his sleeve, and don't you forget it."

Wyatt Earp even went so far as to question Crawford's judgment when the latter came to town to purchase needed supplies.

"Guess I don't have anything to bother about,"

Crawford replied. "Ringo gave me his word he'd get the herd to California, and I reckon that's enough."

"Yes, guess it is," Wyatt admitted. "I ain't got no use for Ringo, but his word is better than most men's bond. If John Ringo told me he was going to walk across the Rio Grande, I'd be there to see him try it."

Curly Bill was hugely delighted with the notion. It tickled the bandit leader's fancy.

"You need a vacation, John," he told Ringo. "For half a peso I'd go with you."

The result of Brocius' enthusiasm was an unlooked for and rather startling development. The morning the drive was to start, Curly Bill and ten of his men appeared on the scene.

"Them fat cows might cause some easygoin' gents to get notions," he told Crawford. "With us along I don't think they'll have 'em. We'll see you to the California line."

Never did a herd cross Arizona so peacefully and profitably. Everybody gave the Rafter S cows a wide berth. They were taking no chances with Crawford's sinister outriders. Usually when a trail herd crosses a holding, the owner of the spread details some riders to make sure none of his cows stray and attach themselves to the herd. But when the subject was broached relative to the Rafter S, there was a bit of a strike among the hired hands. None cared to come within rifle range of the herd. Curly Bill and his men might misinterpret their motives. It is not unlikely that Crawford's herd was considerably augmented before it reached the California line.

They crossed the Colorado, which was low, with little difficulty, and reached the edge of the desert not far from what was to be, in a few years, Needles on the Sante Fe Railroad. It was late evening and the great fiery ball of the sun was sinking into the wasteland and sending glorious rays of multi-colored light over all the vast expanse.

"Don't look much like a desert right now," observed Curly Bill; "it's all covered with flowers."

"Always is right after a heavy rain, which comes darned seldom," Ringo rejoined. "But they won't last. Wither up in a day or two."

Brocius gazed across the mighty wasteland. Despite the carpeting of the delicate-hued thorny vegetation now blazing into flower, the scene had a grim and desolate look. Against the skyline were the blue clouds of mountains, mighty milestones of great distances.

"I'm scairt you may have bit off a considerable mouthful, John," he observed. "You got two hundred miles of burned-over land to cover."

"It can be done," Ringo returned composedly. "I've been across twice and I know where the water is. For instance, just about twenty miles out is a canyon with a creek flowing down it. Water isn't bad, and there's grass and prickly pear and mesquite. Other spots farther out, if you know where to look for them. I figure we'll be okay."

"Hope so," said Curly Bill. "Well, I guess I'll be leaving you in the morning. Don't want to be away from Galeyville too long. Some ambitious gent might figure I was gone for good and get notions."

Ringo nodded without comment. He knew there were warrants out for Brocius in California, and here he did not enjoy the political influence that made him politically immune from arrest in Arizona.

Curly Bill and his men said goodbye the following morning and started on their long ride back east. Ringo watched them till their figures merged with the misty distance. The outlaw's eyes were brooding, his face somber. Perhaps in his dark mind he was thinking that this could be the parting of the ways. Behind him were the turbulent, sinister activities of Galeyville, Tombstone, Paradise and Charleston. Ahead were the clean, austere wastelands, grim, threatening, but uplifting to a man's soul. There, the hot winds blew away the bitterness from one's mind and the rugged mountains inspired calm. It wasn't easy to be petty in the eternal wilderness where the crags and spires stood as tombstones to dead ages. Here man learned to feel and to understand his own significance, shaped by the same hand that molded their terrible greatness. They, too, throughout years by the millions had undergone change, were still undergoing change. They stood as silent witnesses to the unceasing truth that nothing must remain as it is. The wastelands made or broke a man; his was the choice. Just as he could choose the path that led downward into the ghastly sinks that pitted the desert floor, or the road that wound ever upward to the clean and wind-swept heights, so he could rise to the heights or sink to the depths of his own nature. It was for him to make the decision; the wastelands would not make it for him, but they silently pointed the way.

All that day the herd grazed and rested in the shade of trees that lined the bank of a shallow stream that soon lost itself in the desert sands; for Ringo had determined to start the desert drive in the comparative cool of the night.

"By gosh, it is hot!" Crawford remarked as the day wore on. "Reckon it's even worse farther out, eh?"

"Sometimes gets to 125 in the sinks," Ringo returned. "It isn't going to be easy, but I think we'll make it. The worst thing is to get caught in a bad wind storm. We'll have to chance that, though, and we should even win through a bad one if I can manage not to lose my bearings."

The sun went down in flame and splendor. The cowboys rose up and made ready.

"Moon will be up in half an hour," Ringo said as the darkness closed down. "We'll wait for moonrise. Not easy going down these slopes, and we can use a little light."

Finally the moon rose, flooding the wild country with silver light, and throwing a weird sheen on the vast expanse of rolling desert that looked as silent and quiet and alien to man as the star-studded firmament above. The herd got under way.

Sitting his horse as the cows streamed past, Ringo pointed to a tall spire far out on the desert that gleamed wanly in the moonlight.

"We keep that rock in line," he told Crawford. "It don't look so far, but it's close to thirty miles distant. About seven miles this side of it is broken ground and the canyon I was telling you about. We'll bed down in the canyon and start again when the moon rises. I don't figure to do the whole trip at night, but when we have to make a forced march, it'll be better if we've started at night. Well, here comes the drag. Reckon I'll scout up front a bit. You better keep an eye on the wagons and the remuda. Rather rough going down the slopes, and we don't want a wreck to start with."

With a nod to the rancher, he rode along the fringe of the herd, making sure that every man was alert and in his proper place.

Nobody rode directly in front of the herd. Point or lead men rode near the head of the marching column. It was their duty to keep the head of the herd in close formation and to change the course of the column when necessary. Then the riders on one side, riding abreast of the foremost cattle, would veer in the desired direction, while their fellows on the other side would draw away. The leading cattle would swerve away from the horsemen that were approaching them and towards the ones who were receding from them. The point men were carefully chosen for this post of greatest responsibility. They must either determine the exact direction to be taken or follow precisely the route mapped out by the trail boss.

About a third of the way back from the point men came the swing riders where the herd would begin to bend if the course was altered. There the cows would show a tendency to fan out, which must be prevented. Another third of the way back were the flank riders. It was up to them also to prevent straying or sideways wandering.

Bringing up the rear, cursing the dust and the lazy or obstinate critters that tried to hang back, came the drag riders. Nobody liked to ride drag, which was the most disagreeable post. But they were second in responsibility only to the point men.

Following the herd were the remuda of spare horses and the wranglers in charge of them. Last of all came the chuck wagons driven by the cook and his helper, if there was more than one wagon and he had a helper. In this instance, both suppositions were correct.

The trail boss usually rode far ahead to search out water and good grazing ground. But at the moment this was unnecessary. Ringo knew exactly where he was going and had a landmark to guide him. Later, however, as they drew near the canyon, he would lead the wagons on ahead so that the cook could have a meal ready for the hungry punchers by the time the herd was bedded down.

The route Ringo had planned was much the same as that now followed by U.S. 66 to Los Angeles and Santa Monica by way of South Pass, San Bernardino and Pasadena. His objective was the Mojave River not far from Oro Grande, a booming mining town, gold having been discovered in the Old Silver Mountains and the Granite Mountains only a few years before. Here the Mojave was a turgid, muddy stream of respectable size and the range was rich with bunch grass a foot high. Crawford's brother had written that Oro Grande and Mormon Crossing, later to be named Victorville, provided him with a good market for his surplus.

The night was fairly cool, though the atmosphere was thick and heavy, giving a sort of creamy feel to the air, and the herd made good progress. The terrific loneliness of the desert was oppressive. Loneliness and utter silence. The sounds made by the marching herd seemed muted as if fearing to disturb the drear desolation that pressed in on all sides. A point man tried to cheer things up a bit with a song that antedated and perhaps was the basis of one that became very popular years later:

You'd be welcome as the flowers in May,
But still we think you'd better stay away:
For they've built a brand-new jail,
And they open all our mail.
You'd be welcome as the flowers in May!
Still we think you'd better stay away.

But the notes sounded lugubrious in the vast emptiness, and after a couple of choruses he gave it up.

The unevenly sloping, valley-furrowed desert floor was ringed with mountain chains, stark shadows in the moonlight, but under the sun the changing hues—sepia, gray, lavender—would fuse in the distance into a dull blue. The only other variation in the parched, monotonous waste was the glistening salt flats of occasional dry lakes. Cacti reared their rigid, spiny leaves in profusion. Here and there jutted the stark branches of the Spanish bayonet and the Joshua tree.

The general trend of the track was steadily upward. The rise from the eastern edge of the desert to the South Pass was something like 2400 feet. Ahead rose the mighty bulk of the San Gabriel Mountains.

Hour after hour the herd trudged along, bawling protest, snorting and rumbling. The great

clock in the sky wheeled westward. The false
dawn sped across the sky, a pale shadow such as
might be cast by the hovering wings of Death. At
last the east began to blush with primrose. Faint
rays of a deeper rose gradually changed to golden
bars. The stars paled, dwindled to needlepoints of
steel and vanished; the moon waxed wan and her
mountain ridges stood out clear against her sickly
face like the bones on the face of a dying man.
Spears of light flashed across the measureless
wasteland and touched the mountain crests with a
glory through which the dawn glided out upon the
desert. The light brightened, piercing and firing
the veils of haze until the desert was draped in a
tremulous golden glow. The flaming rim of the
sun appeared in the east, and it was day.

Both men and beasts would have been glad to
call a halt, but it was impossible. The heat was
increasing by the minute and all about was an
arid, profitless waste. It seemed to old Sam Crawford that the great spire that was their guiding
beacon was little nearer than when they had
started.

But the rising ground was broken now. Hills
flung up on either side, and finally Ringo pointed
to a shadowy opening between two soaring portals
of dark stone. As they drew nearer they saw that a
sluggish stream flowed from the canyon.

The point men began turning the herd. Their
task was an easy one, for the cows scented water
and made for it.

"Drive 'em up the canyon a way," Ringo directed. "Some trees there, and the overhang provides shade. The water will be a bit better, too."

Fighting the cattle that tried frantically to get to the water without delay, the hands shunted the herd between the gloomy walls of the canyon and kept it going for some distance before they allowed the thirsty animals to plunge their muzzles into the water. The chuck wagons had already forged ahead, and soon the cook had a fire going and breakfast cooking.

The water was nothing to rave about, but at least it was wet, and it made passable coffee.

After eating, the tired cowboys slept in the grateful shade of the overhanging cliffs while the cows fed on the bunch grass that clothed the banks of the stream. There was no need to set a guard, for the cattle would not stray out onto the burning sands.

CHAPTER VI

At sunset the cows were herded out of the canyon and the drive began again; the going was steeper.

"Another twenty miles to some springs in the pass through the Piute Range," Ringo told Crawford. "Then down we go into a section where there is pretty good feed of greasewood and bunch grass. After that there'll be some hard going for a while."

After a hard struggle they reached the pass, just as dawn was breaking. The cacti had become more conspicuous. Most widespread was the chola, the commonest western variety. Ringo eyed the spiny growth with satisfaction. There were also many barrel cacti, stout cylinders sometimes six feet high.

"You can cut the top off them and they yield a fibrous pulp that you pound and get a liquid that quenches thirst," Ringo explained to Crawford. "Many a man has been saved in the desert by the barrels. I don't think we'll need 'em this trip, but the chola is liable to come in handy."

From the west slope of the pass the desert floor seemed to be a fertile plain because of the deceptive greenery of the creosote bush. The trail rounded the hump of the pass. A towering peak, crowned with snow, could be seen in the far distance.

"That's Mount Antonio—they call him Old Baldy," Ringo said. "He's another landmark. We want to keep him in line when we start across that section of burned-over land down below."

The mountain springs that here gushed from under a cliff provided plenty of good water, and there was sufficient grazing to take care of the herd.

The camping site was fully 2700 feet above sea level and it was much cooler. They enjoyed a restful sleep for several hours, after which Ringo started the herd moving again, in mid-afternoon.

"I want to make an early camp on the flats down below," he explained to Crawford. "Bunch grass and greasewood down there the cows can fill up on. Then we've got a tough twenty-mile drive to where a creek of something that looks like water comes out of a canyon. I don't want to chance making that drive in the dark. We're getting into Mojave Indian country now, and they're fighters and always on the lookout for trouble. We'll be lucky to get through without a row. That is, if they spot us, and they've got sharp eyes. A herd like this will be a temptation for a raid. And if they are successful, we won't be around to tell about it. They're killers."

It was around ten o'clock when Ringo called a halt and they made camp by moonlight on the banks of a little stream that apparently came from nowhere and went the same place.

"There'll be ranches around here some day," Ringo predicted. "The vegetation is sparse but it's spread over a wide area. Bunch grass and greasewood provide good fodder, and the cholas help out in a pinch."

"Don't see how the devil a cow or anything else could chaw those spiny things," said Crawford. "They'd tear the mouth out of an alligator."

"You're liable to see how, the next stop," Ringo told him. "For I'm afraid over there chola is all they'll get."

"Hotter down here," Crawford observed.

"Naturally," Ringo replied. "We've descended better than a thousand feet. We'll be down nearly a thousand more when we call a halt next time. Then you'll feel some real heat."

After eating, the hands fell into a sodden sleep from which Ringo aroused them at dawn. The protesting cows were gotten to their feet and there began the hard march over a vast plain sparsely studded with the desert brush. It was a dull-hued land of mystic shades and vistas between bright-colored Clipper Mountains, a jumble of volcanic rock turned brown and yellow by oxidation, and the stark Old Woman Mountains. There was a gradual descent across a bleak, unchanging terrain. Not far off were the yellowish, salt-encrusted flats of Bristol Dry Lake, its drier parts covered by a puffy, powder-like soil into which a man could sink to the knees while he coughed and choked on the stinging dust.

Mirages floated over the lake—castles, cathedrals, what appeared to be great cities and the peaks of mountains. And, aggravating in the extreme, sheets of shimmering water where not a drop of water existed.

The sand was blistered by a temperature well over a hundred, and the beating rays of the sun seemed to scorch the flesh. But to Ringo's relief, the air was still without a hint of wind. A cooling breeze would have been infinitely welcome, but he knew that here no such thing existed. When the air moved it was in roaring, withering furnace-winds that whipped the sand from the desert floor in strangling, stinging clouds.

On every side were low ridges, some of them grown with the withered desert brush. And on these ridges, Ringo's eyes were constantly fixed. The herd was in close formation, the riders alert. Today the chuck wagons would not forge ahead. To do so would be to invite disaster.

Suddenly Ringo, who was riding beside Crawford near the head of the herd, made a low exclamation.

"Did you see him?" he asked.

"Who?" grunted the rancher, rubbing at his sticky eyelids.

"Can't say who, but I'm willing to bet it was a Mojave brave riding just back of the crest of that ridge to the right," Ringo replied. "I caught a glint of sunlight on his rifle barrel. Then where the brush thins a bit he rode up a mite too high and I spotted his dingy white turban. He's keeping tabs on us. I'm afraid we're in for trouble."

"You mean they'll tackle twenty armed men?" Crawford asked incredulously.

"Not out in the open," Ringo said. "If they do, it will be by stealth when they figure they have us at a disadvantage. I figure we can handle them, but it won't do to make a mistake; it will be our last."

All the blistering afternoon Ringo watched the ridges; but he caught no further glimpse of the ominous rider. However, this did not make him feel any better. He deduced that the Mojave had guessed where they were headed and had ridden off to inform his fellows.

But there was nothing the ranchers could do about it. There was only one possible place to bed down, and that none too good. Old Sam shook his head when Ringo called a halt on the bank of a shallow stream that rolled from the mouth of a wide, brush-choked, rock-studded gorge. The water looked like vinegar and had a burning, acrid taste.

"Don't drink too much of it," Ringo cautioned the hands. "It won't kill you, but too much is mighty likely to give you bad belly cramps. We'll boil it and make coffee. That'll be a bit better and less liable to make us sick. Oh, the cows can take it, all right. They'll know when to stop."

c

"But what in blazes are we to do for feed?" demanded Crawford. "There ain't a blade of grass in sight, and that creosote bush ain't no good. And there's nothing else but those infernal chola cactuses. Plenty of them, though, heaven knows."

"Which is fortunate," said Ringo. "I'll show you how to get forage for the cows, thanks to the cholas.

"Break off some dry stuff for torches," he ordered the hands. "Light them at the fire and come along."

The mystified punchers obeyed. Old Sam came along, too, rumbling and grunting. A minute later he was swearing with astonishment.

The bleached chola spines were tinder-dry. A single spark ignited the whole plant, quickly burned off the spines and left juicy green fodder the cows devoured greedily. Little more than an hour's work provided for the needs of the herd.

"Reckon everything is some good if you just know how to handle it," Crawford said with conviction.

"Maybe," Ringo agreed tentatively, "but I'm not sure that applies to a Mojave. We've sure got to handle them right if they show up, good or no good."

Ringo chose the camp site with care, at the foot of a low ledge behind which the ground sloped gently downward.

"Place your bed rolls around the fire, with the

saddles for pillows," he told the hands. "Each man hold out one blanket. And let the fire die down. We won't have to worry about the cows. They're so dead tired they're already lying down, and I doubt if they'll even get up for their midnight stretch. If anything busts loose, there's little chance of their stampeding."

"You expecting trouble, John?" Crawford asked.

"I'm making ready for it," Ringo replied. "In this country, if you don't prepare against possible trouble, you'll be in one devil of a fix if it actually does break. I'm hoping we won't have any, but I'm acting as if we were going to."

As the dark closed down, the hands sat around the fire, smoking and yarning. The weary cows grunted and grumbled and chewed their cuds. The stars glowed large and golden and seemed to brush the distant mountaintops. The moon would not rise until some time later, and the rolling desert land was swathed in grotesque shadows. The cholas brandished their weirdly deformed arms like tortured demons. An intense hush settled over the wasteland, and there was not a breath of air to stir the sands.

The fire died down and the shadows crept closer. The crest of the ledge assumed the look of molten rock that was slowly hardening. Ringo glanced up at the nebulous lip.

"All right," he told his men, "up back of the ledge and spread your blankets there. Go easy and don't make any more noise than you have to. I don't think anybody would be close this early, but it's best not to take chances."

Silently the cowboys obeyed. They were tense, some of them a trifle nervous. The pressing dark, the unearthly stillness, the hint of sinister shapes creeping ever closer through the gloom was a bit trying. Ringo alone appeared not in the least affected. Back of the sheltering ledge he sat without sound or motion, his Winchester cradled across his knees, his somber eyes gazing into the night.

The gaunt crag-fingers of the western mountains pulled down the moon and drowned her in the flood of her own silver tears. The stars burned brighter. The deepening gloom brooded over the wild wasteland like a nesting bird. Nothing blunted the sharp edge of the silence. Even the cattle had ceased their rumbling and muttering. The horses stood with drooping heads. Behind the ledge the tired cowhands dozed fitfully. But the somber-eyed outlaw still sat gazing into the night.

And as the first pale glow of the dawn appeared in the east, a devil's ring of death closed around the silent camp.

CHAPTER VII

Not even the alert Ringo heard them come, those dark-faced killers, their hearts burning with the memory of a thousand wrongs. In the gray uncertain light of the dawn they would take vengeance and reap a fat reward at the same time. They shot greedy glances at the great herd that soon would be theirs, after they had glutted their revenge on the motionless shapes sleeping around the dead campfire. Just a few moments more; let the light get a little stronger, so there would be no mistake.

There was no preliminary warning before the Mojave rifles spat fire. The bedrolls beside the ashes jerked and twitched as the slugs hammered them. A second murderous volley and the Mojaves leaped from their places of concealment and swooped down on the camp with whoops of triumph.

But the exultant yells changed to howls of alarm as the aroused cowboys poured a deadly fire from the shelter of the ridge. Indians fell thick and fast. Those remaining alive fled wildly, with bullets speeding them on their way. The cattle were on their feet, milling and bawling but too weary to stampede. On the ground about the dead campfire lay motionless bodies, seven in all.

"Stay right where you are," Ringo cautioned his men. "Don't move or show a head till the sun's up and I give the word. They're treacherous devils, and cunning. Make a mistake and you'll eat lead. Stay put, I tell you."

The cowboys obeyed the order without question. Through their minds ran thoughts of what would have happened had it not been for Ringo's wise foresight. *They* would have been those motionless forms lying there around the gray ashes of the fire. They had grumbled when he had forced them to sleep on the hard ground with but a single blanket. They weren't grumbling now.

The rim of the sun appeared in the east and swiftly swelled to the fiery disc. But Ringo did not move. He had crouched lower behind the protecting ledge, his eyes never leaving the dark forms sprawled on the ground less than a dozen paces distant. They lay grotesquely just as they had fallen when death struck them down. One was half on his face, his body over the stock of his rifle, the muzzle of which pointed out in front of him. Ringo sat motionless and watched as the heat swiftly increased.

"Stay out," he repeated quietly, and rose to his feet, his thumbs hooked over his double cartridge belts, his hands close to the ivory handles of his guns.

The "dead" brave with the rifle surged to his knees. The black muzzle lined with Ringo's broad breast. But Ringo's hand flashed down and up. The sullen boom of his Colt sent the echoes flying. The Mojave dropped his rifle and pitched forward on his face.

"Guess he's dead this time," Ringo remarked as he slid down the face of the ledge.

"How in blazes did you know he wasn't already dead?" asked Crawford as he hastened to join Ringo.

"Well," Ringo replied dryly, "I never knew a dead man to sweat. This jigger was only creased— see the nick in his scalp? When he came to he decided he'd take somebody with him before he cashed in. I know these people and knew better than to take chances. A wounded Mojave is dangerous as a broken-back rattler. So I decided to make sure none of them were playing possum. When it got hot, the rest of them stayed dry, but this fellow's skin began to shine. Then I knew he wasn't dead and might be conscious and waiting his chance. He was."

Old Sam swabbed his face with his neckerchief. He was perspiring a bit more than even the increasing heat warranted.

"And I was all set to go running down for my horse in case the cows took a notion to scoot," he said.

"You wouldn't have run far," Ringo remarked.

"So I figure," agreed Crawford. "John, guess

we all owe you a mite more than we'll ever be able to pay."

"I was thinking of my own hide, too, when I took precautions, so don't let it bother you," Ringo replied. "Well, might as well get some breakfast. Then we'll move along. Can't risk a night march. Sure hope the weather behaves itself."

"I'd say it ain't behavin' now," a cowboy grumbled. "Sun's hardly up and it's already hotter'n Hades. Don't see how it could be any worse."

"Before the day is over, you may look back on this morning with longing," Ringo told him. "I have a feeling we've got something worse than Mojaves on the prod ahead of us."

He was gazing at the distant mountains as he spoke. From their towering crests strange banners were unfolding, rippling and tossing, sparkling in the sun, a veritable kaleidoscope of changing hues. They advanced and retreated, sank down only to rise upward again.

"That means wind," Ringo told Crawford. "Wind kicking up the snow. If it comes down here we're likely to get a taste of real trouble. Well, there's nothing we can do about it, so let's go."

The herd rolled forward under the burning sun. At first the sky was a hard, brilliant blue, but as the morning progressed the color changed, taking on at first a brassy tint, then deepening to copper. Then, far ahead, they saw what appeared to be a vast wave sweeping toward them. A puff of wind fanned their cheeks but did not cool them. It was dry and hot. Another puff came, hotter than the first. It was followed by others that merged into an ever stronger blast. Through its moan sounded a stealthy rustling that came from all sides. The sands were beginning to move. Another three minutes and the vast cloud of dust rolling out of the southwest reached them. The sky vanished. The sun shone a deep, weird magenta color through the pall of yellow dust. Clouds of flying sand rushed through the air, and grains of gravel. The sand particles stung the flesh like sparks of fire; the swirling dust brought on fits of coughing and a feeling of strangulation. And the heat was increasing by the minute. The vista ahead would be obscured by sweeping, curling streaks and sheets of the dust. Then the gale would roar away, the dust settle and the air clear somewhat. The intermittent blasts were hot as if they poured from a furnace mouth. And even in the moments of comparative calm, high up, the dull yellow pall hung, apparently motionless; and the weird sun, like a red-orange moon seen through haze, grew darker.

Only the plainsman's uncanny sense of direction kept them in the right course. Ringo knew by the increasing air pressure that they were descending into one of the terrible sinks that pit the floor of the Mojave. They were in an eerie abyss of flying yellow shadows, filled with the shriek and moan of the wind. They reached the very bottom of the sink. The pall and roar of the dust storm appeared to be above them. They rode in a strange yellow twilight. The fine siftings of dust were hot and choking; men and animals coughed and sneezed constantly.

"We can't take much more of this," Crawford shouted above the uproar.

"We'll take it as long as we can," Ringo returned. "Got to keep moving. Stop and we'll be buried. Shove the cows along. This sink may turn into a canyon. It should, unless I've got lost or figured wrong. If I'm right, we'll soon be in a gorge that will shelter us, and up toward its head is water, a big spring."

Crawford hoped he was right. For they seemed to be entering the portal of an inferno. The burning heat had the weight of hotly pressing lead. The yellow gloom of dust descended closer and a dim, ghostly light streamed through the shifting veil in which shapes moved as bodiless shadows. Ringo began to believe that he had really lost the way or else had miscalculated the distance. If so, he had a feeling that the clock had just about struck for all of them. No creature could take much more of what they were going through. Already tongues were black and protruding, lips cracked, eyes red-rimmed and almost blind. His body experienced a queer feeling of a lack of solidity, an airy lightness that was disquieting. And despite the intense heat, little prickles of cold ran along his dry skin. The ominous symptoms of approaching heat stroke. He peered anxiously through the murk at the faces of his companions. They were strained, haggard, with sagging mouths and protruding eyes. Ringo was not exactly frightened, but he was badly worried. He rode along the line, checking off the riders, to make sure none had fallen by the wayside. His anxiety was somewhat relieved when he found none missing. But it was clear that they couldn't last much longer. And the terrifying foreboding that always attacks a man lost in a desert sand storm was making itself felt—the crawling fear that he is travelling in a circle.

Suddenly the perverse wind lifted; they could hear it roaring away far above them. The dust still fell, but almost instantly the air was cooler; and the shambling cattle quickened their pace.

"We've made it!" Ringo croaked exultantly through his kiln-dry throat. "The critters smell the water. And we must be in the canyon, and the walls are shunting the wind upward."

He was right. A few more minutes and, as the dust pall thinned, they could make out towering cliffs to the left. Scattered clumps of green vegetation appeared, and scant bunch grass. Then through the hollow roar of the wind overhead came another sound, at first but a faint murmuring. It loudened as they progressed, became a mutter, a low grumbling. A blessed sound—the sound of running water!

The canyon was almost free of dust now, and they could make out the cliffs on the right. They rounded a shallow bend; the cattle broke into a floundering run.

Directly ahead, a body of water gushed from under the cliff on the right, swirled and eddied across the canyon and dived into an opening in the far wall, from the depths of which rose a low thunder. The parched, dizzy cowboys tried to raise a triumphant shout. The result was a dismal, almost inaudible croaking, like the utterances of a bunch of tired frogs with their throats stuffed with cotton. But in another moment, men and animals were taking their fill of the cool, life-giving water.

"Take it easy," cautioned Ringo. "Don't drink too much. Stop while you're still thirsty and wait awhile. Men have died in the desert from over-drinking."

The others took the hint and refrained from following their impulse. Soon they were new men, their skins cool and beginning to sweat, the agonizing raspy dryness leaving their throats. Everybody began to feel hungry. The cook started clattering his pots and pans and Dutch ovens.

Ringo estimated the herd that had already begun to graze. "Didn't lose many," he told Crawford. "A lot less than I feared. The critters were in good shape and could take it."

"Uh-huh, thanks to you insisting that we make night drives," replied the owner. "If they'd already been dried up, they'd never have made it."

The following morning they forded the stream and continued in much better spirits, refreshed by the long rest and ready to laugh at difficulties that had seemed crushing the day before. After a lengthy drive without incident, for the weather had greatly improved, they saw the Sleeping Beauty, a rocky formation resembling a smiling human face, outlined by the crest of the Cady Mountains to the northwest. Here they bedded down beside a trickle of water. The cows munched the sere and scant vegetation, which they seemed to think better than nothing.

Ringo knew he had little to fear from the Mojaves now, having passed beyond their customary haunts, but about fifteen miles farther on was a bad terrain: a six-mile-wide lava field where the clinker would provide hard going for the horses and the cattle. The heat would be terrific and there would be no water until they had passed several miles beyond the field.

Mount Pisgah, an extinct volcano with a deep crater in the summit of its symmetrical cone, loomed ahead. They reached a spot where the landscape, suddenly losing its vegetation, darkened from gray to coal-black. Out onto this forbidding waste they shoved the protesting cows.

"Keep them moving," Ringo cautioned. "This is another fair facsimile of Purgatory."

Everybody agreed it was as the horses floundered over the ribbed and pitted lava floor. The animals were verging on exhaustion when, as the sun was low in the sky, they left the lava behind and mounted a long slope that levelled off onto a mesa where grass grew and there were several good springs. To the northwest lay the glittering salt-encrusted bed of Troy Dry Lake.

"Shouldn't have much trouble from here on," Ringo told Crawford. "We're past the worst of it. Next bedding-down place will be under the cliffs of Newberry Mountains. Good springs flowing from under the cliffs and plenty of grass. Wouldn't be surprised if that section turned to farming and fruit raising some day. We've got a couple of stretches of real desert still to cross, but they're comparatively narrow. The rest of it should be sort of a pleasure jaunt after what we've been through."

In a way it was. Day after day they marched on across the endless, sandy plains, watching the sun rise, watching it reach its zenith, watching it sink again. Night after night they ate their simple food with appetite and slept beneath the glittering stars till a new dawn broke in glory from the bosom of the east.

Ringo spoke little during this time. It was as if the silence of the wastelands had affected him and sealed his lips. He seemed to live in a kind of dreamland, thinking perhaps of the past, reflecting much upon the innumerable problems of the passing show called life, and not paying much heed to the future. What did it matter to him, who never knew whether he should have a share of it for another month or even a week, living as he did in the shadow of death? Perhaps he reflected upon the state where past, present and future would be one; and these reflections, which were in their essence a kind of unshaped prayer, brought a modicum of peace to his storm-tossed soul. For years he had lashed his soul with bitter thoughts, lest he forget the past and find peace. Days he had consecrated to remorse, to regret, suffering, to punishment. He had refused to take any joy from the life he had recklessly thrown away. But here in the mighty calm that set at naught man's hopeless strivings and passions, something greater than himself pressed its infinite hand down upon him and forced him, for the moment, to forget self and partake of the vast tranquillity the desert had to offer. Perhaps if he had stayed in the desert, grand, lonely, the abode of silence, untainted by life or corruption, the bitterness would have been washed from his heart and his life turned from that dark bourne to which it was destined to brighter and more sunlit channels. But he missed the infinite truth, and with his own hands closed the gates.

Finally they sighted Shadow Mountain and crossed the Helendale Yucca Mesa. The yuccas were really trees, deformed, weird, bristling, shaggy-trunked, with grotesque shapes like specters in torture. Many of them bore large white flowers streaked with pink, and here they were fresh and green. Ringo loved them. Perhaps their twisted branches seeming to writhe in torment reminded him of his own wracked soul that was in sympathy with the strange desert trees. Such thoughts come to a man on the moon-blanched desert under the spectral-armed yuccas.

Another stretch of desert; then wide-spreading sycamores and spire-like poplars and the muddy flood of the Mojave which flowed here the year round. They allowed the tired cattle to feed on the rich, foot-high bunch grass and then moved on. Soon they were passing bunches of cows that stared at them in mild-eyed wonder.

"Good-looking stock," Ringo commented. "Tamer and easier to handle than our longhorns."

Old Sam gazed at the fat cows with bright eyes. "Yes, and they're wearing my brother's Cross C brand!" he exclaimed exultantly. "John, we're on our holdin's. Must be getting close to the *casa*."

Two more miles and they sighted a sprawling white ranchhouse set in a grove of sycamores. Horsemen were riding toward them, yipping and shouting. Another minute and Crawford was shaking hands with his brother's grizzled range boss, who welcomed him heartily and was evidently glad to be relieved of the responsibility of running the spread.

Ringo spent a week with Crawford, helping

him to get things in shape and resting after the arduous march.

"But why leave me, John?" Crawford protested. "There ain't no sense in you going back to that hell-hole over there. This is a good holdin', and it's a nice country. Understand you have kinfolks a bit farther west. You could visit 'em often. You'd do well here. Besides," he added, "I ain't getting any younger and I've got nobody in the world. I'll have to leave the spread to somebody when I pass on. Why shouldn't it be you? Stay with me, John. I brought all my books along, and there's many good ones you'd like to read. And we can always find a lot to talk about. You'd be happy here."

Why Ringo turned down this chance to start a new life is a mystery. He gave no reasons, merely thanked Crawford for his generous offer, declined it, and rode back east. He arrived at Galeyville bronzed, clear-eyed and in splendid physical condition. Otherwise, he appeared to have changed not at all. The old somber expression shadowed his fine-featured face and he was even more taciturn than before. Once more he was Lucifer, Star of the Morning, fallen from high estate.

Curly Bill welcomed Ringo with boisterous enthusiasm. "Was getting scairt maybe you'd run out on me," he said. "Things ain't seemed the same since you been away. Lots of things been happening, too. Wyatt Earp figures to run for sheriff against Johnny Behan. Bet he don't beat him. Russian Bill and Sandy King got themselves hung over in Shakespeare, New Mexico. Bill stole a horse. King shot up Shakespeare twice a week and folks decided he was a nuisance that had bcttcr be got rid of. They hung 'em in the dining room of the Pioneer Hotel. Folks were mad as anything because dinner was late. Blaine Wilson got in a fight with Wyatt Earp and Wyatt pistol-whipped his head open."

"Wyatt Earp is a cold proposition," Ringo commented.

"You can say that twice," admitted Curly Bill. "I hate the man, but I ain't denyin' he's got guts."

CHAPTER VIII

Somebody, several persons, in fact, tried to hold up the Benson stage. In the strongbox was eighty thousand dollars in gold. It would have been a nice haul, but things didn't work out right. The bandits killed Bud Philpot, the driver, and Peter Roerig, a passenger who was riding on top of the stage. When Philpot fell from the seat, he dropped the reins and the horses ran away down a steep grade, left the road and plunged through mesquite and over rocks. Bob Paul, the shotgun messenger, who had emptied both barrels of his weapon at the outlaws, managed to retrieve the reins and finally stop the runaway. The coach was riddled with bullets but Paul was untouched. The bandits got nothing.

All of which was a rather routine matter in Cochise County annals. The rumor that was bruited about after these happenings was not routine. The story was spread that Doc Holliday had taken part in the abortive holdup. Holliday denied it, and so did the Earps, but the rumors persisted. Finally Holliday was actually arrested. Wyatt Earp bailed him out and the case was eventually dismissed for lack of evidence.

This unexpected development was of decided interest to John Ringo and Curly Bill. Even though nothing had been proven against Holliday, the fact that their chief henchman was under a cloud did the Earps no good. People who had been convinced that Wyatt would beat Johnny Behan in the race for sheriff and had been prepared to support his candidacy were now dubious about his chances.

"Johnny's in the saddle," Brocius exulted, "and so long as he runs the county, we're sitting good. I tell you, John, the Earps are on their way out."

They were, but the last pages of the story would be written in blood.

After Curly Bill finished speaking, Ringo sat silent for some time. Unlike the impulsive and carefree Brocius, who saw only immediate advantages in the discomfiture of the Earps, Ringo looked to the future. His keen mind evaluated what he had learned and arrived at a singularly accurate conclusion.

"Yes, Bill," he said slowly, "the Earps are on their way out, but so are we."

Curly Bill stared in astonishment. "What the devil do you mean by that?" he demanded. "Ain't Johnny Behan our friend? I tell you we're sitting pretty. Johnny will beat Wyatt in the race for sheriff. He'll be elected hands down."

Ringo slowly shook his head. "You are right

in that Wyatt Earp will not be elected sheriff,"
he replied. "Fact is, he won't even be here to
run. But don't fool yourself; Johnny Behan will
never be elected sheriff again either. Just like
Wyatt, he won't even be here after the election.
Johnny will pull out, too."

"Why—why—" Brocius sputtered, "Johnny's
settin' on top of the world."

Ringo permitted himself the shadow of a
smile. "Mighty slippery on top of the world,"
he said. "And always a lot of folks around with
pries to topple you off your perch. The higher
up a man gets, the easier a target he becomes,
and the more vulnerable. A man has to have
clean hands to hold up on there. Johnny's are
a mite sticky, and we might as well admit it."

Brocius grew thoughtful. "John," he admitted,
"perhaps you got something; but little Bill don't
figure to get squashed when Johnny tumbles off
his perch. Why? 'Cause he aims to be out from
under. And," he added impulsively, "I figure
to take you out from under with me. We'll talk
about that some other time. Got other things to
talk about right now. The boys are getting a
mite short on cash and are restless. We've got
to figure something."

One development of that conference sent Jake
Gauze, Milt Hicks, John McGill, Jack Mc-
Kenzie, Bill McGill and Bud Snow riding into
Mexico. Gauze and his companions were the
ablest cow thieves of Curly Bill's band. Born

cattlemen, they knew all the tricks, and had perfected them by much practice.

"A small, compact bunch can handle such a chore better," Ringo explained to Curly Bill. "Let them make the raid; we'll stand back to be in reserve in case trouble develops."

Trouble did develop, plenty of it.

The party rode deep into Mexico, nearly a hundred miles, by way of lonely trails known only to the outlaw fraternity. Near the Border the ranches were so well guarded that raiding them had become hazardous. Ringo figured, and rightly, that farther south the Mexicans, anticipating no trouble, would take fewer precautions. Gauze and his men finally reached a big ranch where they ascertained that the herds were left unguarded at night. They studied the lay of the land and had little difficulty cutting out three hundred prime beef critters and running them north. Everything was rosy until they were close to the Border. Then what had been little more than a profitable pleasure haunt through the hills turned into a grimly serious business. A roving vaquero spotted them and hurried away to get help. Gauze and McGill, riding drag, saw behind them the glitter of steel as the hard riding van of more than a score of vaqueros closed in.

Old hands at the business, the two cowboys let the Mexicans get within easy rifle range before they opened fire. They emptied a couple of saddles but the Mexicans kept coming. They were close on the heels of the herd when the cattle plunged bellowing through the San Luis Pass and out into the Animas Valley. Here, under ordinary circumstances, would have been safe sanctuary. But the circumstances were not ordinary. Gauze and his companions gave up the unequal fight and split the wind for Curly Bill's Roofless 'Dobe Ranch only five or six miles distant. The triumphant Mexicans speeded them on their way with bullets and then turned the cattle, lined them in a column and headed back south.

John Ringo, Brocius and about half a dozen others were playing poker when the discomfited raiders dashed up with their story of failure. The outlaws were filled with righteous indignation. By some distorted process of reasoning they felt that they had been robbed of what was rightfully theirs. The Mexicans had stolen their cattle! They set out on the vengeance trail without delay. Ringo headed the "posse" straight for the San Luis Pass, figuring correctly that the Mexicans would make for the gap in the mountains. As they raced their horses across the valley they saw the rising dust cloud that marked the position of the herd. Shouting with excitement, they quickened the pursuit.

The Mexicans saw them coming and pushed the cattle as hard as was possible. Where they made their mistake was in not abandoning the cows and riding for safety. They decided to fight a rearguard action. Since their pursuers were outnumbered about two to one, the vaqueros doubtless felt they would be able to hold them at bay until the cattle were pushed across the Line where they could count on assistance. The decision was a fatal one for nearly half their number.

Just inside the wide jaws of the pass the outlaws got within shooting range. They opened fire at a gallop. The Mexicans fired back. But they were up against men to whom shooting from the back of a racing horse was routine business. Vaqueros fell at the first volley, and continued to fall. There followed a grim and deadly running fight through the hills. Belatedly the Mexicans abandoned the herd and tried to find safety amid the rocks and gullies. One by one they were ridden down and slaughtered. With the approach of night Ringo ordered a halt to the killing.

"We don't know what's riding up from below the Line," he told the others. "We'll be at a disadvantage in the dark. Liable to be surrounded. Get those cows rounded up and headed back into the valley."

Brocius seconded the order. The victorious outlaws got the bewildered herd turned again and ran it to the Roofless 'Dobe. Fourteen, perhaps more, Mexicans had been killed. The outlaws suffered only a few minor casualties.

When the outlaws got back to the ranch, they

found Old Man Clanton there with several of his hands and neighbors, including Dick Gray, Billy Lang, Bud Snow, Harry Earnshaw, and Dick Crane.

Bread cast upon the waters returns again many-fold, says the Bible; but the "bread" John Ringo cast upon the waters when he allowed the sole survivor of the Skeleton Canyon massacre to escape was to return bitter fruit for the Brocius outfit. The young Mexican, who lost two brothers in the slaughter, seethed with a desire for vengeance. He kept unending watch on the outlaws he had recognized, including Old Man Clanton. Perhaps Clanton's vicious face had impressed itself the most strongly on his memory. Anyhow, it was later learned he singled out the saturnine ranch owner as his particular target for revenge. So far he had not been able to get at Clanton. But opportunity was in the making.

The morning after the thrice stolen herd was brought to the Roofless 'Dobe, Old Man Clanton inspected the cows with a speculative eye, stroking his snowy beard with a gnarled hand.

"Bill," he said, "tell you what I'll do: I'll give you fifteen dollars a head for 'em. I can sell 'em in Tombstone. What say?"

Brocius glanced at Ringo, who nodded. "Okay," said Curly Bill. "It's a deal. Save us the trouble of disposing of 'em, and we need money to keep the poker game going. John and

Joe Hill, the sharks, have just about cleared the rest of us."

Clanton paid for the cows on the spot. He had come to the Roofless 'Dobe prepared to make a purchase, feeling sure that the raiders would not return from Mexico empty-handed. He took his time about moving the herd, figuring to bed down first in Guadalupe Canyon. Not until the next day did he set out on the drive that would cross the Guadalupe Mountains by way of the canyon and thence to San Bernardino Valley, Sulphur Springs Valley, and around the Dragoon Mountains to Tombstone. Everything would be hunky-dory and he would dispose of the cows at a nice profit.

But meanwhile Jim Hughes and Tall Bell had jaunted over to the nearby town of Gillespie and in a saloon loquaciously discussed the whole business, including the sale to Clanton and the old rancher's plans. Pleasantly mellow, neither noticed the slender Mexican youth at a nearby table with his steeple-crowned sombrero drawn low over his eyes and his *serape* muffled up about his chin. The shadow of the wide hat hid the exultant gleam in the dark eyes as the *muchacho* greedily drank in the words of the two outlaws. He attracted no attention when he got up and stole furtively from the saloon. Outside, he quickened his pace till he was almost running when he reached the rack where his horse was tied. He cantered out of town and, once well in the clear, sent the cayuse south at a furious gallop. His heart was singing with triumph. At last he would have his chance at the bewhiskered old devil who had killed his brothers. South of the Border he quickly rounded up an intrepid band of kin of the men massacred in Skeleton Canyon. They rode north through the hills until they reached Guadalupe Canyon, where they made their plans with care and waited.

Clanton and his men were expecting no trouble. They were on their home grounds, and nobody would dare to meddle with members of the Brocius outfit. The Mexicans had been soundly thrashed just a couple of days before, and the survivors of the fight in San Luis Pass were doubtless licking their wounds and thankful to be there to lick them. The killings in Skeleton Canyon were water over the dam, and it was doubtful if Clanton and the others ever gave them a second thought. So they blithely shoved the herd into Guadalupe Pass as the lovely blue dusk was sifting down the slopes like impalpable dust. Their plan was to bed down at a spring not far inside the pass. They close-herded the cows and then, in the deepening dusk, gathered about the campfire to prepare the evening meal. And in the thick brush on the gloomy slopes above the camp, the Mexicans leveled their rifles and took careful aim. Old Man Clanton stood stroking his beard and warming his back by the fire.

A muttered word of command and nearly a dozen rifles spat fire. One wild, triumphant yell rose above the crackle of the guns as Old Man Clanton fell backward into the fire, and rolled over once, scattering sparks and embers in every direction. Dick Gray leaped into the air with clutching hands, as if seeking to grasp his own escaping soul, and fell dead beside Clanton. Jim Crane pitched forward on his face. His body jerked and writhed as bullets hammered it. Billy Lang went down to lie without sound or movement. Bud Snow ran for the shelter of the brush but was riddled by slugs before he reached it. Earnshaw, who had intended to ride " Killpecker," the night guard trick, from sundown till eight o'clock, had left saddle and bridle on his horse. By some miracle he was untouched. He forked the plunging bronk and rode madly for the canyon mouth. A well-aimed bullet brought his horse down. Earnshaw landed in some brush and was only scratched and bruised. He scuttled away through the growth and holed up in a dense thicket where he lay praying that his enemies would not discover him. They didn't.

As the darkness deepened, the Mexicans stole down upon the silent camp, rifles ready; but there was no need for caution. The silence continued—the motionless silence of death.

The Mexican boy spat in Clanton's bearded face. He dipped his finger in the rancher's blood and drew a crimson cross upon his forehead—

the brand of Cain! Then the triumphant band rode south with three hundred fat beeves in addition to their glutted vengeance.

Earnshaw lay hidden for hours. Then he set out on foot for the Cloverdale Ranch, which he reached the next day in a state of extreme exhaustion.

John Ringo, Curly Bill, and others rode to the canyon and brought in the bodies for burial. Ringo's eyes were more than usually somber as he gazed at the dead men.

"Five of our best," he remarked to Brocius. "Bill, I have a feeling this isn't the end, either. Wonder who'll be next?"

And as he spoke, it seemed to Brocius that a pale shadow flickered on Ringo's handsome face, such a shadow as might fall from Death's advancing wing. The outlaw chief was not an imaginative man, but suddenly he felt cold all over.

The Clanton boys swore vengeance, and it is said that thereafter whenever they found a lonely Mexican out on the range they tortured and killed him. At any rate, thirty-eight known dead was the final tally of the massacre in Skeleton Canyon.

CHAPTER IX

It was not long afterward that John Ringo took his celebrated stand for the orderly process of law.

Jim Wallace was a fairly new member of the Brocius outfit. It was said he was a horse thief from New Mexico and had come to Arizona when the territory to the east got too hot to hold him. He was a sullen, argumentative type and was considered dangerous. In Phil McCarthy's saloon at Galeyville he got into a dispute with Curly Bill over Deputy Sheriff Billy Breckenridge. Brocius flew into a rage and knocked Wallace down. Wallace got to his feet slowly, wiping the blood from his face.

"I ain't no match for you with fists and I know it," he said quietly. "But I'll be waiting outside."

Had Wallace flung that challenge at the cool, composed Ringo, he would have been dead in sixty seconds. But Brocius was impulsive and given to blind rages. For a moment, being about half drunk, he didn't get the significance of what Wallace said and stared after him with a puzzled expression on his face. Ringo offered some well meant advice.

"Let him go, Bill," he said. "He's drunk. There's no sense in this sort of foolishness. We've got enough to contend with without fighting among ourselves."

If Ringo had not spoken, Brocius might not have caught on and his attention would have perhaps turned to some other drunken vagary. But abruptly he understood. His face turned a dark red, and the cords of his neck swelled. With a roar of anger, he shook off Ringo's restraining hand and dashed for the door.

When Curly Bill rushed out, spewing profanity and going for his gun, Wallace was standing in the street beside his horse, a forty-five in his hand. Some people maintained that Wallace was sheltered behind his horse and was aiming the gun across the saddle. But Ringo, who saw it all, said no, Wallace was standing in the open. He shot from the hip.

The bullet grazed Brocius' jaw, sliced off a hunk of meat and knocked him down, stunned. Wallace glanced inquiringly at Ringo.

"I've no desire to kill you, Jim," Ringo said quietly. "So far as I can see it was a square fight. Bill isn't hurt much and there's no sense in this thing going further. Fork your bronk and ride off for a while till things cool down."

Wallace was about to do so when the town marshal came running up and demanded that he surrender his gun and submit to arrest. Pretty well sobered up by what had happened, Wallace obeyed without protest. The marshal locked him up in the little calaboose preparatory to taking him before Justice Ellingwood and having him bound over. Ringo assisted the cursing Brocius to his feet, took him into Babcock's saloon and dressed his wound. Still considerably shaken, Brocius lay down in the back room and immediately went to sleep. None of Curly Bill's immediate followers other than Ringo was in town at the time, so Ringo returned to the bar, thinking the incident closed.

It wasn't. The sullen and quarrelsome Wallace was not popular with the town folks. The openhanded, genial Brocius was. A garbled story that Wallace had shot Brocius in the back from ambush travelled like wildfire. Knots of angry citizens gathered in the street, especially in front of Jack Dall's saloon which quickly became the focal point for the various groups.

An excited man came running into Babcock's. "They're goin' to hang Wallace!" he shouted. "They're getting together down at Dall's place. They already got a rope. Yeah, they're goin' to string him up."

"That so?" remarked Ringo, and walked out of the saloon.

Ten minutes later the mob, fortified with plenty of red-eye, headed for the jail. The marshal came out and tried to quiet them. He was seized and disarmed. Yelling and cursing, the mob rushed forward, then abruptly halted.

A second man had appeared from the interior of the building and stood lounging in the doorway, thumbs hooked over his double cartridge belts.

"Guess that's about far enough, boys," John Ringo said quietly. "You're not going to hang Wallace today. It was a square fight. Bill isn't hurt much and he can take care of his own feuds. Get going!"

The mob didn't like it. They cursed and hurled threats. "Get him!" somebody in the rear shouted.

Ringo smiled contemptuously as his somber eyes centered on the front rank.

"Guess you can get me, all right," he said. "There are fifty of you. But I'll get four or five of you before I go down. Who wants to be the first?"

Nobody seemed particularly obsessed with the desire. They realized the cold fact that Ringo was perfectly ready to die, and the equally cold and uncomfortable fact that he wouldn't die alone. Doubtless they didn't deduce what Wyatt Earp had shrewdly surmised when Ringo had challenged him to shoot it out in the street—that here again was a convenient way for John Ringo to commit suicide; but they did understand perfectly that it was a certain way for somebody else to commit suicide. Perhaps they didn't consider self-destruction moral or ethical. Anyhow, they hesitated, cursing and muttering.

D

Ringo swept them with a contemptuous glance, deliberately turned his back on them and walked back into the office in front of the cells. Nobody followed him.

The would-be lynchers spent the rest of the afternoon explaining to one another why they had let Ringo get away with it. Wallace was duly bound over but disappeared soon afterward and was never tried. When Curly Bill woke up he laughed over the whole episode, swore because laughing hurt his sore jaw, and began discussing the details of a proposed holdup with Ringo.

The holdup, when it came off, was due to cause another clash between Ringo and Wyatt Earp. Just why there was such constant warfare between these two outstanding individuals is hard to explain. Some might say it was the instinctive aversion of a peace officer for a confirmed outlaw. But that explanation hardly suffices. There is little question but that Doc Holliday was at least on the fringe of outlaw land; but just the same, Wyatt Earp was his firm friend. Wyatt also liked Buckskin Frank Leslie, his head bartender, and if Leslie wasn't an owlhoot he missed being one by the skin of his teeth.

No, it went deeper than that. The two men had much in common. Both were cold, calculating, absolutely fearless, complete masters of their emotions in times of stress. No matter how hectic the moment, their brains functioned without a hitch. They evaluated conditions exactly and acted with hair-trigger speed. They seldom if ever made a mistake when analyzing an opponent, and both had an uncanny ability to anticipate an adversary's move.

In other ways they were the antithesis of one another. Wyatt was the exponent of law and order, methodical, exact, cast in the mold of his father's fathers and conforming to the plan laid out by them, desirous of advancement, looking to the future. The opinion of his associates and society in general meant much to him and he governed his actions accordingly.

Ringo was strictly the individualist, nonconforming, intolerant of all restrictions, abiding by no rules of conduct other than those ordained by his own stern but eccentric code of ethics, utterly indifferent to the opinions of others. He was without ambition and without a goal, content to look out upon the passing show of life from the oasis of his own lonely personality, taking little interest in events except when they challenged or interfered with the accepted order of his own existence. In fact he took little interest in anything, perhaps because of indolence, perhaps because he was sufficient unto himself. It is doubtful if he was capable of strong emotion of any kind. Wyatt Earp would follow the vengeance trail with cold, suppressed fury, undying hatred and inexorable persistence. Ringo wouldn't take the trouble. He would brush obstacles aside and forget them. He held no malice for an injury done him. It is doubtful if he ever hated anyone. He would unhesitatingly kill a man who was in his way, but would not step aside to pursue one who had been an obstacle in his path. He considered it a waste of time and effort. His allowing the Mexican youth to escape the massacre in Skeleton Canyon was an example of his attitude. The chore of ambushing the train and securing the silver had been done. Ringo had no interest in the lone escapee and saw no sense in taking the trouble to shoot him, which he would have done instantly had the boy been an obstruction.

The two men were as outstanding personalities as the West ever produced. One was to die in blood in the flower of manhood, the other to die in bed at the age of eighty-four.

John Ringo planned the Charleston silver brick robbery, as it was called, and worked out the intricate details. The participants in the affair were Ringo, Curly Bill, the McLowery brothers, Joe Hill, and Pete Spence.

Because of a scarcity of water in the Tombstone district—although they were to have a great deal more than they wanted later on—the stamp mills of the Tombstone Mining and Milling Company were located at Charleston, on the west bank of the San Pedro River. Day and night the air of Charleston quivered to the pounding and thunder of the great stamps doing their ceaseless dance. Upright rods of iron as large as a man's ankle, and heavily shod with a mass of steel and iron at their lower ends, were framed together like a gate, and these rose and fell, one after another, in a ponderous dance, in an iron box called a battery. Each stamp weighed six hundred pounds or more. The ore was shoveled into the battery and the steady movement of the stamps pulverized the rock to powder. A stream of water that trickled into the battery turned this into a creamy paste. The minutest particles were driven through a fine wire screen that fitted close around the battery box.

The particles were washed into great tubs warmed by super-heated steam. These tubs were called amalgamating pans. The mass of pulp in the pans was kept constantly stirred up by mullers. A quantity of quicksilver was kept always in the battery, and this seized some of the liberated gold and silver particles and held onto them; quicksilver was also shaken in a fine shower into the pans, through a buckskin sack, about every half hour. Quantities of coarse salt and sulphate of copper were added from time to time to assist in the process of amalgamation by destroying the base metals which coated the gold and silver and prevented it from uniting with the quicksilver.

At the end of the week the machinery was stopped and the pulp gotten out of the pans and the batteries. The quicksilver with its imprisoned precious metals was molded into balls which were put into an iron retort that had a pipe leading from it to a container of water. A roasting heat was applied to the retort. The quicksilver turned to vapor, an oily black smoke that escaped through the pipe into the container where the water turned it into quicksilver again. From the retort was taken a lump of pure silver, white and frosty-looking, with a certain gold content that did not show in the coloring. This was melted and poured into a mold to produce a solid brick of silver weighing around 250 pounds.

An intricate and tedious process, but the result was something to cause the mouths of road agents to water.

John Ringo had had his eye on the silver shipments for some time. His fertile brain finally evolved a scheme which he hoped would procure some of the bricks and at the same time put Wyatt Earp on a hot spot. The Wells Fargo Express Company handled the shipments, which in consequence came under Wyatt's jurisdiction.

The plan involved the services of two puddlers —men who cast the silver into bricks and were not averse to making a crooked dollar.

The shipment of silver bricks left for Benson early in the morning. Beside the driver perched a shotgun guard, more for show than anything else, for what road agent would be so foolish

as to try to make off with the heavy ingots? His
horse would be bogged down in less than a mile
and a hard-riding posse would overtake him with
little difficulty.

So the guard was highly astonished when, from
the brush where the road forked, rode four
masked men with the familiar command of,
"Hands up!"

The guard instinctively started to raise his
shotgun. Curly Bill shot him. But, strange to
say, Brocius did not kill him. The man who
could knock the tops off beer bottles at thirty
paces merely wounded the guard in the arm.
The shotgun clattered to the roadway as the
guard clutched at the injured member with a cry
of pain. The more discreet driver was already
"up," both hands reaching hard for the sky.

"Down off that and help unload," ordered
Curly Bill.

The driver obeyed with alacrity. The groaning guard also clambered painfully from the
seat. Curly Bill motioned him to one side. "You
ain't no good for anything but to beller," said
the outlaw chief. "Shut up! you ain't more'n
scratched." He raised his voice in a shout:

"Okay, Pete; bring her out."

A light wagon drawn by two horses clattered
from concealment. It was driven by a fifth
masked man, Pete Spence.

All except the watchful Brocius dismounted
and went to work on the shipment. Grunting and

swearing, they transferred the hefty bricks to the wagon. Then, after a cheerful goodbye to guard and driver, they headed the vehicle down the fork of the trail that wound due south to the Mexican Border. Where the trail curved through tall brush, one of the outlaws turned off a moment, to reappear leading a fifth horse, saddled and bridled.

The wounded guard was still cursing and groaning, but the driver was all excitement. "Tom," he exclaimed, "the outlaws forgot to shoot the horses. Wait. I'll tie a rag around that arm—it's just a meat wound—and then I'm headin' back to town. I'll get Wyatt Earp and a bunch and they'll run the hellions down long before they get across the Line."

He suited the action to the word, cut loose one of the stage horses, mounted it bareback and sent it speeding for Tombstone. Ten minutes after the driver rode his lathered mount into the silver city, Wyatt Earp and his posse were on the trail.

In addition to the three Earps, Wyatt, Morgan, and Virgil, the posse included Doc Holliday and Frank Leslie, both staunch Earp men. In the light of what followed, Wyatt could not have made a more unfortunate selection.

The posse sighted the wagon from the crest of a rise a short distance from the scene of the holdup. It was standing at the bottom of the long slope and nearly two miles distant. The eagle-eyed Wyatt counted five men grouped around it. Over to one side stood a clump of saddled and bridled horses.

"Looks like the sons are having trouble of some sort," Wyatt exclaimed exultantly. "Let's go!"

At top speed they thundered down the slope. Soon it became apparent that their approach was noted by the outlaws. The white blobs of faces turned in their direction. There was a drawing together of heads, then a concerted rush for the horses. A moment later the last owl-hoot had vanished into the brush. The wagon heaped with the metal ingots still stood motionless, looking very small and lonely in the vast desolation.

Minutes later the posse pulled their blowing horses to a halt beside the wagon.

"A wheel came off," Wyatt exclaimed. "Reckon they had to hunt for the hub cap— there it is lying in the road where they dropped it."

"We riding after them?" Morgan asked excitedly.

Wyatt shook his head.

"Guess not," he decided. "They've got a head start, and the chances are they know the lay of the land, and we don't. Mighty little chance of catching up with them, and they might manage to lose us in that badlands over there, circle back and grab off the wagon. No, we'll just take the stuff back to Charleston. Now I wonder what loco hellions tried this fool trick, anyhow?"

"Who else but the Brocius bunch?" said Holliday.

"Don't you believe it," Wyatt answered. "Trust John Ringo and Curly Bill not to make such a fool try. It was some brush-popping outfit with mighty little savvy. Even if their wagon hadn't busted up, we'd have caught 'em before they made the Line. If it had been the Brocius bunch, there wouldn't have been any horses left alive for the driver to ride to town. Mighty good chance neither the driver nor the guard would have been left alive, for that matter. Ringo and Brocius don't fool when they're on a job."

"The driver swore he recognized Curly Bill's voice," insisted the argumentative Holliday.

"He *thought* he recognized it," corrected Wyatt. "It's got so that whenever something is pulled in this section, everybody recognizes Curly Bill in one way or another, even if Bill is fifty miles away at the time setting in the middle of town with folks all around him. It's got to be a habit with guards and drivers. Well, screw that cap into place, Morg, and let's head back for town. We did a good chore. The mill manager will get a surprise."

The mill manager did, but not exactly as Wyatt had figured.

With Morgan driving the wagon, the posse made a triumphant entry into Charleston. The mill manager bustled out to greet them, smiling and rubbing his hands together. He shook hands with Wyatt, congratulated him on his exploit. Then he turned to the wagon to check the tally of the bricks.

Suddenly he halted, staring. His face turned purple; he seemed to breathe with difficulty. His eyes glared and watered as he turned them on the puzzled posse members, who were noting these alarming symptoms with bewildered concern. But he did not address them directly at the moment. He beckoned to a group of laborers busy nearby.

"Unload that stuff, carry it into my office and stack it," he ordered in a choked voice.

The laborers obeyed, struggling with the unwieldy ingots that appeared to be uncommonly heavy. When the last brick was deposited, the manager motioned the posse into his office. He closed and locked the door. Then he exploded.

"Lead!" he roared. "What's the idea, anyhow? Lead!"

The posse stared in bewilderment. "Lead?" Wyatt repeated. "What the devil you talking about, Austin?"

"Lead!" stormed the manager. "Bars of lead frosted with a little white paint to look like silver. Any fool with one eye could see that. That is," he added with meaning, "if he was honest."

For once Wyatt Earp was taken aback. His

jaw dropped. He blinked at the wrathful manager. The other's implication struck home and he flushed angrily.

"Austin, are you trying to say that ain't silver?"

"Yes, I'm trying to say that ain't silver!" the manager mimicked with vicious sarcasm.

Wyatt's face darkened even more. "And you're intimating that—" he began.

"I'm intimating nothing," the manager interrupted. "I'm *telling* you that thousands of dollars worth of silver is missing and in place of it you bring me a wagonload of rubbish worth a few cents a pound. How in blazes do you think we are going to explain this to Wells Fargo and collect our insurance? They'll fight us through every court in the land, and beat us."

Wyatt was speechless. He examined the bricks closely, cut into one with his knife. There was no gainsaying the manager: the bars were lead.

"Looks like it was the Brocius bunch after all," Doc Holliday observed cheerfully.

Wyatt turned on him with an oath. "You don't have to rub it in," he said. "We were outfoxed, that's all. Blast John Ringo, anyhow! Let's get out of here."

The crestfallen posse filed out, followed by the black looks of the plainly suspicious manager.

And at about that moment, the jubilant outlaws were gleefully retrieving the silver bricks from where they had cached them in a thicket loading them into a second wagon and heading for the Mexican Border. Later there were high old times in Galeyville, Charleston and Paradise.

Strange to say, the Tombstone papers made no mention of the ludicrous affair. *The Epitaph* ran a short item on the robbery and the recovery of the loot, and that was all.

"There's Wyatt Earp's hand," chuckled John Ringo. "Doubtless he persuaded the mill manager to hush the thing up, pointing out that if what happened became generally known, some other enterprising galoot might try the same thing."

Nevertheless the story got around by word of mouth, and didn't do the Earp faction a bit of good.

CHAPTER X

As an aftermath of the affair, Wyatt Earp, doubtless for the first, last and only time in his life, went off half-cocked, with resultant additional discomfiture for himself and the others. He got word that Curly Bill was alone in Charleston, blind drunk and boasting of the robbery.

"I'll get that hombre and throw him in jail for robbery and make the charge stick," Wyatt vowed. "The stage driver and the guard will swear it was Brocius pulled the job."

"It doesn't sound good to me, Wyatt," objected the more canny Virgil. "Their testimony will 'pear a bit shaky when a good lawyer gets through with it. Goodrich will defend Brocius, and he's a tough man."

But the furious Wyatt was beyond reasoning with. "I'll chance it," he said. "I have an appointment with Dick Gird that I can't put off, but I'll finish with him in a hurry. It's eleven o'clock; be ready to ride by three."

Bill Leonard heard what Wyatt said. He slipped out of the Oriental Bar, unnoticed, and rode at top speed for Benson where he knew John Ringo was spending the day.

Ringo listened quietly to the story gasped out by the breathless Leonard.

"Get me another horse while I saddle my critter," he said. "Chances are I'll need two if I'm to beat Wyatt and his bunch to Charleston."

Ringo did need two. He rode his own mount to a standstill and finished the journey on the second. When he arrived in Charleston, he found Curly Bill asleep and blissfully unaware of what was in the wind.

Wyatt, Virgil and Doc Holliday rode for Charleston at a leisurely pace. They passed Robbers' Roost and the old Brunckow mine. They emerged from the hills, and Charleston lay before them on the far bank of the San Pedro. They rode to the bridge, and halted.

At the far end of the bridge stood a tall man with a rifle cradled in the crook of his arm.

"Guess that'll be about far enough, boys," John Ringo called.

Wyatt and his companions considered the situation. It was far from satisfactory. Ringo was in a strategic position. He was partially shielded by a post. The sun was at his back and dazzled the eyes of the posse. Wyatt arrived at an eminently sensible conclusion.

"You win, John," he called, "but we'll be seeing you."

"So long, boys," Ringo called back affably. "Come around any time you're of a mind to."

Afterward, Wyatt justified his decision.

"I wasn't particularly scared of Ringo," he said, "but I wasn't ready to die just then, and I knew I would die if I tried to cross that bridge. John Ringo hits what he shoots at."

Wyatt maintained that Ringo was the deadliest gunfighter the West had ever produced, and Wyatt was not given to making rash statements. Ringo was not accorded the reputation enjoyed by other experts simply because he was no exhibitionist. He never indulged in trick shooting. Blowing the cigarette from Curly Bill's hand at their initial meeting was the only incident of the sort on record, unless shooting the "Man from the Pecos" through the mouth might be considered one. Doc Holliday would shoot at nail-heads, and sometimes hit them. Curly Bill specialized in knocking the tops off beer bottles. Buckskin Frank Leslie used to "paint" his wife's portrait with a six-gun. Standing her against the wall with her profile turned toward him, he would outline her attractive face and form with bullet holes in the wall. Tiring of this genteel pastime, Mrs. Leslie finally divorced the "artist."

Ringo, on the contrary, went in for no such dallying. He reserved his skill for men.

A fair estimate of Ringo's deadly accuracy may be garnered from an incident that occurred in Babcock's saloon. A New Mexico gunslinger named Opper, with considerable of a reputation as a fast-draw man and killer, picked a fight with Ringo. Later, when Opper's body was examined, he was found to have three bullet holes in his chest, just over the heart. A silver dollar would have covered all three holes!

It is not illogical to assume that the bitter hatred Wyatt Earp had developed for John Ringo was at least indirectly responsible for the bloody events that were soon to follow. Wyatt's hatred extended to all Ringo's associates and focused particularly on the two McLowery brothers, Frank and Tom, and the Clantons, Ike, Billy and Finn. The unsavory quintet were vocal and did their bragging wherever they could get somebody to listen. They boasted about how Ringo had put it over on the Earp posse in the matter of the silver robbery and had then forced Wyatt and his companions to back down at the Charleston bridge. They also predicted what would happen to the Earps eventually if they continued to buck Ringo and Curly Bill.

It was not all vapid talk. Back of the braggarts was a grim and powerful criminal organization that sprawled over a good part of Arizona, its fringes extending into New Mexico. The Earps were supreme in Tombstone—Wyatt and Virgil had pretty well cleaned up the town—but outside, in Cochise County, it was John Ringo and Bill Brocius who called the plays, with the sheriff and other law enforcement officers very largely puppets on the strings they manipulated.

Characteristically, it was the utterly fearless Ringo who voiced a word of caution.

"Finn," he told the oldest Clanton, "you're needlessly looking for trouble, and if you don't watch out you'll find it. You can push Wyatt Earp just so far. All this fool talk doesn't get you anything, and first thing you know it's going to be put up or shut up—draw or drag—and either way you've got nothing to win and everything to lose."

"We're going to run the Earps out of Tombstone," boasted Ike Clanton, the big talker of the bunch.

"Maybe," Ringo conceded, "but you can count on it, before you finish the chore, Wyatt and his bunch will run some of you straight to Boothill."

Ringo's warning had a sobering effect for a while. The Clantons and McLowerys kept out of Tombstone.

Ringo's advice was sound. As long as the Brocius outfit left the Earps alone, Curly's men had little to fear from them. Virgil was marshal of Tombstone, his jurisdiction covering only the town. Wyatt, a Wells-Fargo employee, had been appointed a deputy United States marshal, his authority limited to federal offenses. Johnny Behan, the sheriff of Cochise County, was complacent if not actually co-operative. Wyatt Earp was not a man to go looking for trouble, and if he had not been goaded into a cold fury by the

Clantons and McLowerys the chances are he would have let the Brocius bunch alone, contending it was Behan's job to enforce the law throughout the county.

One of John Ringo's outstanding characteristics was patience. He could plan a foray down to the minutest detail, and then, if necessary, take days or even weeks to carry it to a successful conclusion. Also, he was wont to stray farther afield than his associates in outlawry, who preferred for the most part to operate as close as possible to headquarters. The robbery of the Oatman bank was an example.

Oatman was a mining town in the blue-shadowed foothills of the Black Mountains. Its one street was built on a long hillside with stores, saloons, dance halls and other buildings in an unbroken row. In front of the stores was a wide plank boardwalk raised on stilts at the lower end to make it level and reached by flights of wooden steps. Wooden awnings on the store fronts shadowed the shop windows. The settlement was named for a pioneer family that had been attacked by Apaches near Gila Bend in 1851; the parents were killed, a boy beaten senseless and left for dead, and two girls were captured, one to die in captivity, the other to escape later. This was an inauspicious beginning for a settlement, to be sure, but when gold was discovered in the Black Mountains and the foothills, Oatman prospered. Ringo had passed through it in the course of one of his trips to California and had been impressed by the little town's affluence and its isolated situation. So much so, in fact, that he had spent some time in its environs, familiarizing himself with the surrounding territory and the trails in and out of the hills. In Oatman John Ringo saw opportunity.

The town had a single bank, rather isolated at the end of the street. Later, when three million dollars' worth of gold would be taken from the vicinty in three years, it would have two, along with ten stores and a chamber of commerce, and a narrow-gauge railway extending from the nearby mines to Fort Mojave on the Colorado River, to which point a ferry brought supplies from Needles, California.

For his expedition to a far corner of the state, Ringo chose for his companions Joe Hill, Frank Stillwell and Pete Spence, men of tried courage and above the average in intelligence.

The officials of the Oatman bank were a watchful, suspicious lot. An alert guard paced the little lobby. The cashier was an old Border fighter, and the tellers were chosen for their efficiency with hardware as much as for their ability to add up a column correctly. So it was not remarkable that they eyed askance the four riders in rough and dusty mining garb, booted and spurred, heavy guns swinging at their hips, who hitched their horses at the rack across the street and approached the bank.

Upon entering the bank, three of the new-comers paused inside the door, glancing about with interest. The guard edged into a strategic position, and the tellers kept their right hands below the counter.

The fourth man, a tall, auburn-haired individual with dark, somber eyes, walked to the cashier's window with an assured step. He dropped a plump buckskin poke onto the counter.

"You handle dust, don't you?" he asked in a deep, slow voice.

"Why, yes," replied the cashier.

"Then we'd like to deposit this poke with you," said the stranger. "Some shady characters roamin' about in the hills these days, and we don't feel safe packin' our pokes on us."

His suspicions somewhat allayed, the cashier weighed the gold dust and wrote a deposit slip for the amount. The tall man pocketed it with a nod. "Hope we'll see you soon again," he said, and walked out, his companions stringing along behind him.

"That's a hard-looking bunch, Cale," the guard remarked to the cashier.

"They're that," agreed the cashier, "but I reckon they're all right. They deposited a bit over seven hundred dollars worth of dust."

The four "miners" loafed about town for a couple of hours, had a few drinks, purchased some staple supplies and rode off into the hills.

Five days later they were back, this time with more than eight hundred dollars worth of dust.

The next week the performance was repeated. The fourth time they appeared at the bank they had considerable more than a thousand dollars' worth of gold, including several small nuggets.

"You boys seem to be doing pretty well," remarked the cashier as he wrote out the deposit slip.

"Oh, not bad," the tall man admitted. "We ain't going to get rich, but it beats riding for forty-per-and-found. A couple more weeks and we ought to have enough for a nice bust, if our luck holds."

"Would be better to leave most of your money here at interest," the cashier counselled.

"You may have a notion there," John Ringo agreed. "We like to get interest on our money."

The cashier did not appreciate the grim humor of the remark.

The fifth time the outlaws appeared at the bank, about an hour before closing time, nobody paid any attention to them. The guard nodded cordially and transferred his interest elsewhere. The two busy tellers kept right on figuring in their cages.

The cashier glanced up from the deposit slip he was writing, and looked squarely into the muzzle of John Ringo's ivory-handled six-shooter. The two tellers were similarly accommodated by Stillwell and Joe Hill. Pete Spence had his gun barrel jammed against the guard's back.

"We've come to get that interest on our money," Ringo remarked affably.

The bank employees were lined against the back wall, their hands in the air. Pete Spence held a gun on them while Ringo, Hill and Stillwell, with the efficiency and dispatch born of much experience, cleaned out the vault and the cages. Then the employees were herded into the vault and the door slammed shut. Only the timely arrival of a depositor saved them from death by suffocation.

By the time the bankers were released, the town aroused and a posse gotten together, the outlaws had a head start and night wasn't far off. In the darkness the posse lost the trail, never to recover it.

It was said that the exploit netted the outlaws better than a hundred thousand dollars in coin and gold dust.

CHAPTER XI

Ringo's daring exploit replenished the coffers of the band, but nothing else good came of it. Bereft of his restraining hand, the Clantons and McLowerys returned to Tombstone and made trouble. Ike Clanton got drunk and had a violent altercation with Doc Holliday. A story had been started by somebody that Ike Clanton and Frank McLowery had revealed to Wyatt Earp the names of the men who had taken part in the attempted Benson Road stage robbery in which Bud Philpot was killed; that they had put the finger on Jim Crane, Bill Leonard and Harry Head. A certain credence is lent to the tale by the fact that Ike Clanton and Leonard had had a vigorous dispute over the ownership of a ranch both claimed. When the story finally broke, Leonard, Head and Crane were all dead. Crane had died when the Mexicans ambushed Old Man Clanton and his bunch in Guadalupe Canyon. Leonard and Head had been killed by Ike and Bill Hastings at Owl City, New Mexico. But all three were living when Ike Clanton was supposed to have made a deal with Wyatt Earp relative to reward money.

The story was believed by some, denied by

others. An argument can still be started in Cochise County over the matter, although all concerned have been dust for many years.

But even though the purported victims of the conspiracy, if there was one, had passed on, it was a deadly serious matter for McLowery and Clanton. If the outlaw fraternity believed the story, their lives were not worth a busted peso, and they knew it. So it was not surprising that both, whether they were falsely accused or the victims of a double-cross, flew into a towering rage and vowed vengeance. Ike Clanton hunted up Wyatt Earp, and told him all about the alleged conspiracy. Wyatt denied it. Ike said that Doc Holliday had told him it was so. Holliday said that Ike was an infernal liar and that he intended to tell him so the first time he saw him. Ike did not believe what Wyatt told him. He proceeded to spread the story that Leonard and Head had told him the Earps and Doc Holliday were connected with the Benson Stage holdup, and that now that Leonard and Head were dead, he feared that the Earps would murder him because of what he knew.

The Earps and Holliday were also in a bad spot. The Clantons and McLowerys, their own lives in danger, would be out to get them. The outlaws would feel that it was absolutely necessary for their own safety that the Earps and Holliday be gotten out of the way. There was only one sure method of silencing them. So the two factions were at daggers' points. The final outcome of the unholy mixup was the bloody battle in the O.K. corral, in which three men died. But that was later.

The grand row between the Clantons, the McLowerys and the Earps occurred while Ringo was absent on his expedition to Oatman. When he returned to Galeyville, he found the trouble kettle boiling furiously.

Ringo was disgusted with the whole business. "It's the sort of thing that gets you nothing and loses you everything," he told Brocius. "I don't see why you allowed those fools to get out of hand."

"It all happened before I got wind of it," Brocius defended himself. "Ike Clanton is a windbag; I don't think anybody will pay attention to his blowing."

"That's where you're wrong," Ringo answered. "The Earps have enemies who will jump at a chance to discredit them. This row will give them a talking point, and you can expect them to make the most of it."

"I sure ain't going to worry my head about what happens to the Earps," said Curly Bill.

"Okay," replied Ringo, "but something bad will happen to some of our boys before this is finished." The remark was prophetic.

The Earps hated John Ringo, and as far as they were capable of fearing anything, they feared him. But while they had nothing but contempt for the Clantons and McLowerys, they held Ringo in high respect.

"It's a shame that a fellow who has everything like John Ringo should be riding a crooked trail," Wyatt once remarked to Doc Holliday. "I can't understand it."

"Funny things happen to a man," Holliday replied reflectively. "Take me, for instance. If I hadn't gotten mixed up in a fool shooting when I was a young fellow, the chances are right now I'd be a respectable dentist back in Louisiana. But I did get mixed up in one and had to cut and run. I understand something of the same sort happened to Ringo. And then other things come along to keep you going." He coughed as he spoke, wiped his lips with a snowy handkerchief and drew it away, showing the bright crimson stain of arterial blood.

"See what I mean?" he said, tossing the bloody handkerchief into a nearby spittoon. "When your body is sluffin' off to nothin', an inch at a time, you get funny notions and don't give a darn about much of anything. And you get a feeling you want to get even with something. You don't know just what, but you hanker to get even. I got a notion Ringo is in much the same pickle as me."

"There isn't anything wrong with Ringo's body," Wyatt grunted.

"Nope," agreed the consumptive Holliday,

"but there's plenty wrong with his mind. I figure Ringo's mind is just like my lungs, slowly rotting away. Time'll come, and it won't be long, when my lungs'll all be gone. And just the same thing will happen with Ringo's mind. When my lungs are gone, that'll be the end of me, and when Ringo's mind is gone, that'll be the end of him. Mark what I tell you. I figure it's sort of a race between him and me as to which goes first. I'll die in bed. Ringo won't."

Holliday once told Ringo, half jovially, half in earnest, "John, I just can't understand how a first-class rustler and gunslinger like yourself got mixed up with a bunch of cheap brush poppers."

Ringo had replied, "Doc, I'm blamed if I know myself!"

Trouble was breaking fast and furious. Two bandits attempted to rob the Charleston plant of the Tombstone Mining and Milling Company. It turned out to be a murderous fiasco. The masked bandits, without warning, shot and killed M. R. Peel, the company's chief engineer. Then, apparently frightened at what they had done, they ran from the office with empty hands. They were tentatively identified as Zwing Hunt and Billy Grounds. Deputy Sheriff Billy Breckenridge and a posse descended on a ranchhouse where the two men were staying. There was a fight and Grounds was killed, Hunt wounded and arrested. Hunt never came to trial. He was placed in a hospital from which he escaped. He was supposed to have fled to Mexico with his brother, Hugh Hunt. Anyhow, he was never seen again. Rumor had it that he was killed by raiding Indians, but this was never definitely established.

The ominous result of the various happenings was the steady thinning out of the Brocius gang. One after another the most loyal and capable members were being eliminated. And more were soon to go.

In those days the standing of rustlers and bad-men was unique. Just as saloon keepers or pro-fessional gamblers were not looked upon as undesirable citizens, except by certain elements, usually in the minority, so wideloopers and pro-fessional gunfighters were often estimated for their personal attributes. As a rule they were brave, dashing men, generous, open-handed, loyal to the death, the best of friends.

So it was not remarkable that peace officers did not always find the citizenry solidly behind them.

All of which helped John Ringo, Curly Bill Brocius and their associates to go their rollicking way. In view of the political influence they en-joyed, about the only way to stop them was with the six-shooter. And it was the six-shooter, used frequently and accurately, that finally ended the reign of Ringo and Curly Bill.

Lethal doses of "lead poisoning" had already

made serious inroads. Old Man Clanton, Dick Gray, Billy Lang, Sandy King, Russian Bill, Bud Snow, Jim Crane, Billy Grounds, Zwing Hunt, Bill Leonard, Harry Head and others were gone. All had been trusted and capable members of the band. Some—Clanton, Gray and Lang, for instance—had been able to boast a certain aura of respectability, being owners of ranches and other property. Gradually the topmost lieutenants were being eliminated, leaving those with the reputation of living only by outlawry; but these were the deadliest and most ruthless. The Brocius gang was still something to give pause to the boldest.

Tom Hayes, Lafe Burley, Jackson Fry and Bert Childers plotted to rob the Shakespeare, New Mexico, bank. While not so well known as others, they were among the more capable of Curly Bill's retainers. The plan was well thought out, every detail apparently considered, no hazard overlooked.

But somebody talked, and the sheriff and the citizens of Shakespeare were ready for them. All four were killed.

Next, Joe Hill and Jake Gauze stole a valuable racing mare which they expected to sell for a good price in Mexico. They didn't. While trying to escape a pursuing posse, Hill's horse fell with him and broke his neck. The posse overtook Gauze and cheerfully hanged him.

"Bill," John Ringo said somberly, when word

of the latest fiascos reached Galeyville, "there aren't many of us left."

"Not so many as there used to be," Brocius admitted, "but so long as we've got the Clanton boys and the McLowerys and Frank Stillwell and Pete Spence and Indian Charlie and Hank Shelling, we aren't doing so bad."

"Billy is the only one of the Clantons worth a hoot," observed Ringo. "Finn is slow and stupid, and Ike, for all his big talk, is a coward. And Bill Murphy has to go and get his neck broken when *his* horse falls with him. Bill was a good man, and dependable."

"That's right," Brocius agreed. "And Cary Raines has to go and get himself hanged down around Sonoita for hoss stealing. Cary was a good man, too. Yep, quite a few of the boys have taken the Big Jump lately. Wonder who'll be next?"

"I wonder," said Ringo, his eyes brooding.

Which ended the conversation that both men doubtless felt had already gone on too long.

Events were shaping up to a climax faster than Brocius or even Ringo anticipated. It was Ike Clanton, the drunken braggart, who precipitated the showdown. Ike's hatred for the Earps was vocal at all times, more so when he was in his cups. Ike rode to Tombstone, got roaring drunk and proceeded to tell all and sundry how he aimed to kill Wyatt Earp and Doc Holliday. Thus Ike raised the curtain on the bloody drama the last act of which, though few guessed it at the time, would be the end of the Earp's reign in Tombstone, and the twilight hour of the Brocius gang. The climax of the play was a roaring gun battle in which Billy Clanton and the McLowery brothers were killed.

The aftermath of the fight was turmoil. Certain factions declared that Holliday and the Earps had murdered the three cowboys in cold blood. And there were those who predicted that the friends and relatives of the slain men would exact bloody vengeance.

These last were right. Not long after the conclusion of a legal battle in which the Earps and Holliday were vindicated—white-washed, their enemies said—Virgil Earp stepped out of the Oriental saloon and was cut down by a blast of shotgun fire from the darkness. He was left a cripple and in no condition to resume his duties as town marshal. Partially recovered, he departed for California. A little later, Morgan Earp was killed from ambush. Wyatt and Holliday were left alone, but ready to ride the vengeance trail.

Morgan Earp's killers were supposed to have been Frank Stillwell and Indian Charley. Four days later Stillwell's body was found near a railroad crossing in Tucson. And very soon afterward, what was left of Indian Charley was discovered in a thicket on Pete Spence's wood ranch. Wyatt Earp and Doc Holliday were blamed for the killings. Their position in Tombstone was now untenable.

The two grim men began disposing of their properties and making methodical preparations to leave Arizona forever.

CHAPTER XII

Empires crack before they crumble, and the first cracks seem easily mended.

To all outward appearances, Curly Bill Brocius was sitting pretty. His two great enemies, Wyatt Earp and Doc Holliday, were definitely on the way out. They were making preparations to leave Tombstone and Cochise County forever. Johnny Behan, his friend, was still sheriff. Tombstone was booming, too busy enjoying its prosperity to give much thought to the outlaws in the hills. And without active support from the powers of wealth and influence in the silver city, the outlying ranchers could not hope to cope with organized outlawry.

But just the same Curly Bill did not feel right. Perhaps as he conned over in his mind the long list of those "fallen by the wayside," he wondered anew who would be next. There were many graves, some in boothill cemeteries, some out on the lonely prairie, some where only the growing grass sought to cover the moldering bones. And each of these graves was the last abiding place of one who had been high in his councils, a tower of strength in time of trouble. Frank and Tom McLowery, Billy Clanton, Sandy King, Joe Hill—

the list was unpleasantly long. Who would be next? Curly Bill sat in moody thought, and thought of that sort in large doses is apt to prove depressing.

"John," he said suddenly to Ringo, "how'd you like to go down into Mexico—way down into Durango?"

Ringo shook his head. "Was down there," he replied. "Didn't like it."

"I did," Brocius said. "Liked it fine. Met a lot of fine people down there. One old Don especially. He was a grand old feller. Owns a ranch about the size of Arizona, and more cows than you can shake a stick at. Lives in a great big house with rooms about the size of the Crystal Palace saloon, all full of fancy furniture and doodads that cost a fortune. Servants to wait on him; fifty of 'em, maybe more. When you sat down at his table, there was so much first class chuck you didn't know where to start in. And drinks! None of the tanglefoot whiskey we have to guzzle. He's got a cellar full of wine so old the bottles are growin' whiskers. And the best horses you ever laid eyes on. He took quite a shine to me and wanted me to stay on with him. When I rode away he begged me to come back some day and never leave again. Got a cute little daughter, too, purty as a spotted pony. I think she sort of took a shine to me, too. Anyhow, them big black eyes of hers sort of filled up when I said goodbye. *She* didn't say 'goodbye.' She just said, "*Hasta Luego!*'"

"'Till we meet again!'" Ringo translated.

"That's right." Brocius nodded. "Looked like she figured I'd come back some day, and sort of wished I would. I dunno, John! I dunno! Everything looks good right now, but somehow I don't feel just right about the way things are going."

Ringo nodded sober agreement. "I don't, either," he admitted. "The Earps are on the way out, but just between you and me, I've got a notion Johnny Behan is on the way out, too. We're likely to get a man in the sheriff's office we can't talk to. Say a man like John Slaughter."

"That snake-eyed hellion!" exploded Brocius. "Nobody can talk to him. He's pizen, and I mean plumb pizen. We sure couldn't get very far with John Slaughter if he was sheriff."

"Judging from the talk I've been hearing, that's just what he's liable to be," said Ringo.

Brocius sat silent for some moments, gazing steadily into the purple-misted south where the mountains of Mexico were like a blue pencilling against the skyline. He passed his stubby fingers through his curly black thatch.

"I dunno!" he repeated. "I dunno!"

On the morning of March 21, Wyatt Earp and Doc Holliday had completed their preparations for leaving Tombstone. They had a last drink together in the Oriental Bar. The white-coated Frank Leslie served them in silence but with his unfailing courtesy. Nobody ever knew exactly where Buckskin Frank stood in relation to peace officers and outlaws. He made friends with both, was cordial to both, reserved with both. He was a silent man with an unfathomable, furtive mind. Neither friends nor enemies could ever guess just what Buckskin Frank was thinking about. He said goodbye forever to Wyatt and Holliday, with whom he had been closely associated for years, as casually as if merely passing the time of day. Wyatt and Holliday were more solemn with their adieus. They were pretty sure that never again would they meet with Leslie in this world. Draining their glasses, they walked out of the Oriental saloon and mounted their horses. Waiting in the saddle were young Warren Earp, recently arrived from California, where he had been living with his parents, Sherman McMasters, Texas Jack Vermillion, and Jack Johnson. All had been followers of the Earps in their day of power and still clung to them even though their star was no longer in the ascendancy.

At a walk they sent their horses along Allen Street, which was thronged with people, some their friends, some their deadly enemies. No word was spoken, no hand raised. A curious silence blanketed the crowded street, as if those who watched felt that they were witnessing the end of an era. As a matter of fact, they were, the end of an era of courage, bloodshed, drama, tragedy and sordidness. The Earps were leaving

Tombstone, and soon Tombstone would change from a roaring boom town to a lonely hamlet in the shadow of the hills.

Standing where Allen Street became Sumner, John Ringo watched the Earp party reach the edge of town and increase their horses' pace to an easy gallop.

Westward the land was bright. But out of the east a great cloud was rising in the blue spring sky. Up and up it rolled, purple and piled and heavy with evil. And as it climbed higher and higher, a dark shadow crept slowly across the prairie toward the town built on a granite spur that resembled the outstretched paw of a crouching lion. It touched the hills of silver, drew nearer, stealthy, ominous. Westward the land was bright, but in the east the darkness deepened as if it were night. A strange hush fell. No bird sang. The leaves hung motionless on the trees. The cloud climbed higher; the shadow crept on and on. Tombstone was swathed in gloom, an unearthly twilight that was infinitely depressing.

To John Ringo's imaginative mind the thing was symbolic, prophetic. Far to the west, Wyatt Earp rode onward in the sunshine; rode on to a new life, achievement, success, and peace. Tombstone lay in the shadow. Ringo turned away and with bowed head walked slowly to his horse.

Iron Springs was a fine waterhole in the Whetstone Mountains. It was about thirty-five miles west of Tombstone, on the route taken by Wyatt Earp and his companions. As it happened, Curly Bill Brocius, Pony Deal, Milt Hicks, the Lyle brothers, Ed and John, Frank Patterson and Bill Johnson were resting at Iron Springs in the shade of a bank some four or five feet high. They were hidden from the trail. Their horses stood nearer the waterhole, where the shelving bank was much higher, and were also invisible from the trail. The outlaws were smoking and yarning with no thought of danger. Suddenly Pony Deal cocked his head in an attitude of listening. "I hear horses," he said.

"Some of the boys, I guess," Curly Bill replied carelessly. "I rather expect John Ringo and Curt Hume will be riding down this way today."

The hoofbeats of the approaching horses grew louder.

"Sounds like five or six fellers," remarked Ed Lyle.

Curly Bill levered his bulky form from the ground. He peered over the lip of the bank. For an instant he stood as if turned to stone.

"It's Wyatt Earp and a whole bunch of men! Look out, boys!" he yelled, and drew his gun.

The outlaws leaped to their feet, clutching their rifles. They levelled them across the bank and opened fire.

The Earp party had pulled up less than twenty yards from the bank. As bullets screeched around them, all but Wyatt whirled their horses and rode madly to get out of range.

Wyatt had his Wells-Fargo shotgun and ammunition belt looped to his saddle horn. With the utmost coolness he drew the shotgun from the sheath and, with lead whistling past him, cutting his sleeves, ripping the flare of his britches, he raised the weapon and took steady aim at Curly Bill. All the outlaws but Curly Bill ducked behind the bank before the threat of the yawning twin muzzles.

Bill was aiming at Wyatt. The two men pulled trigger at the same instant. Wyatt sat erect in his saddle, but Curly Bill reeled back with a cry of pain, tripped over Milt Hick's foot and fell to the ground, groaning and cursing. Wyatt turned his horse and rode to join his companions, bullets storming after him.

Frank Patterson knelt beside the cursing leader. "You hurt bad, Bill?" he asked anxiously.

"Heck, no!" sputtered Brocius, with a string of oaths. "The galoot just nicked a hunk of meat from my shoulder. Did you get him?"

Patterson shook his head. "We threw everything we had at him," he replied. "We might as well have been using spitballs for all the good it did. He just kept right on riding."

A queer, strained expression crossed Curly Bill's face. "The bullet ain't run that can get him!" he muttered. "Shootin' at him is just a waste of time. And maybe he ain't gone for good.

Maybe he'll come back sometime. Boys, I don't like it."

He fell silent while Patterson tied a handkerchief around his buckshot-gashed shoulder.

"I don't like it," he repeated, buttoning his shirt. He rose to his feet and stood for a moment brooding. Then with purposeful steps he strode to his horse and mounted. He glanced around, then turned the animal's head south toward where the mountains of Mexico lay against the sky.

"So long, boys," he said.

"Where you goin', Bill?" Pony Deal called after him.

"So long, boys," Brocius repeated, and quickened his horse's pace.

Silently they watched him ride away; watched as his figure grew small and blurred, merged with the purple mist and vanished from their sight forever.

CHAPTER XIII

The departure of Curly Bill spelled the end of the Brocius gang as a compact and powerful organization. John Ringo did not take enough interest in his associates to hold them together and direct their movements. He went his own moody way and let them go theirs.

But the activities of groups and individuals did not cease with the passing of Curly Bill. It was the veritable heyday of rustling. A stream of longhorns was pouring in from Texas. Aggregations of capital such as the Heart-Haggin interests of California, the Denver-owned Red River Cattle Company, and the Aztec Land and Cattle Company, to name only a few, were attracted by the lush grass and ideal climatic conditions of the San Simon and other broad and fertile valleys ringed about by sheltering mountains. They proceeded to set up in business. But soon the wideloopers became so active that some seriously considered going out of business.

The erstwhile followers of Curly Bill took an active part in the depredations. They were old hands. They were familiar with all the hidden trails through the hills, and the mountain hideouts. And they knew where the best markets on both sides of the Border were to be found. So they went their merry, tragic, sometimes heroic ways.

The outlaw belongs to a strange and contradictory breed. Ruthless, vicious, seemingly without a spark of good in his onery carcass, he sometimes rises to the heights of sheer generosity, stark heroism or amazing self-sacrifice. The examples are legion. When the pastor of a Tombstone church desired an ornate fence to surround his church and there was no money with which to pay for it, the outlaws of Galeyville heard of the good man's dilemma, took up a purse and sent it to him anonymously. The preacher got his fence and never knew that it was paid for by the outlaw fraternity. Buck Fanshaw was a robber and a cold killer, but when he heard some hoodlums were desecrating a small Catholic cemetery, he took a pick handle and waded in, knocking out several of the miscreants and putting the rest to flight. Then he sat down on a headstone, rolled a cigarette and waited. As fast as the unconscious recipients of his attentions recovered their senses, he put them to work repairing the damage. Buck was not a Catholic nor, so far as anybody was able to ascertain, did he have or had he ever had religious affiliations of any sort. Buck just thought what was being done wasn't right.

Hank Porter, a badman of more than local repute, heard that a Mexican was very sick with smallpox and that nobody dared enter his cabin to care for him.

"Reckon not even a oiler had ought to be treated that way," said Porter. In the face of warnings and dire predictions, he took over the job of looking after the sick man and successfully nursed him through the dread disease and back to health.

"Smallpox? Shucks!" said Porter. "When I walked in the door every pox there, little ones and big ones, went out the window pronto. They weren't takin' no chances with Hank Porter. No, siree! Smallpox, shucks!"

Even more outstanding was the act of little Johnny Upshaw. Johnny was a cowhand who had a respectable record as a rustler and stage robber. One night his employer, Shane Price, was playing cards in a Charleston saloon. Price accused a crooked dealer of cheating. The dealer pulled a sleeve gun and prepared to dispatch his accuser. Johnny Upshaw deliberately stepped in front of Price and took the slug intended for the ranch owner in his own chest. Then he took the gun away from the dealer and shot him through the head before he collapsed. John Ringo risked his life to save Curly Bill from the vengeance of the Mexican *vaqueros*, and risked it again to save from mob violence the man who had wounded Curly Bill in a fight. So Lafe Gulden's behavior was not without precedent.

Many strange characters passed through Galeyville from time to time; none stranger than Lafe Gulden.

Gulden was a lance-straight little man with pale eyes, a tight mouth, and sharp, pointed, milk-white teeth. In appearance he somewhat resembled a weasel, and in disposition he was a veritable prototype of the ferocious little bloodsucker. He had made considerable of a reputation for himself in New Mexico as a cold killer who feared nothing that walked, crawled or flew. Where he hailed from originally nobody knew, and Gulden wasn't saying. Texas was generally conceded responsible.

Gulden might have proved a valuable addition to the Brocius gang except for the fact that he and Curly Bill just couldn't hit it off. Whenever they got together sparks flew, and it was freely predicted that the smoldering feud would end in a killing. It doubtless would have had it not been for the restraining influence of John Ringo over Brocius.

"Let him alone," Ringo counselled. "The man's mad and not responsible for what he does. No sense in wasting lead on that sort. Let him alone."

Ringo himself had no use for Gulden and let Gulden know it. As for Gulden, he kept away from Ringo. It was unlikely that he was afraid of Ringo or anyone else that lived; but, like Wyatt Earp, he wasn't ready to die just yet and he knew he would die if he tangled with the passionless killer.

Be that as it may, Gulden, to all practical purposes, committed suicide when he killed Billy Brooks, the head bartender at John Turner's saloon across from Babcock's place.

Billy Brooks was a quiet, elderly man of considerable education. John Ringo liked him and liked his company. They would sit together for hours discussing books and other matters that were so much Sanskrit to the rest of the Brocius bunch. With the exception of old Boone Logan, Brocius and young Billy Clanton, Brooks was about the only person in Galeyville Ringo wasted time on.

What he drank never showed outwardly on Lafe Gulden. He remained the same lance-straight, neatly dressed, poker-faced individual no matter how much alcohol he consumed. But inwardly, after a certain number of potations, he became a venomous reptile. He was in just such a mood the night he walked into Turner's saloon and got into an argument with Brooks over change. Gulden declared he hadn't received change from a twenty-dollar gold piece. Brooks said he had.

Brooks was courteous but firm. Gulden waxed vehement, and threatened the old bartender. Brooks merely smiled.

That smile apparently did it. Gulden pulled his gun and shot Brooks dead. Then, perhaps realizing that he had gone a bit too far even for Galeyville, he mounted his horse and rode out of town, fast.

There was some talk of getting up a posse and following him, but it ended in talk.

John Ringo was away at the time, on a protracted drinking bout in Tucson, Bisbee, Tombstone and other places. Billy Brooks had been dead and buried a week when he got back to Galeyville.

When he heard of the cold-blooded killing, Ringo went into a cold fury. He set out to run down Gulden, just as, years before, he had set out to run down his brother's killers. Ringo was riding the vengeance trail again, and he wouldn't give it up till Gulden or himself was dead.

When Gulden left Galeyville, he drifted over to Pima County, joined up with a couple of kindred spirits and set up in business for himself. He proceeded to cut a considerable swath.

The authorities of Pima County liked it not at all. Pima County was plenty woolly, and they had trouble enough on their hands without Gulden. Augustino Chacon, the Mexican raider, was just coming into power, and he had chosen Pima County for his base of operations north of the Mexican Border. How Chacon was outwitted and captured by Captain Burton Mossman of the Arizona Rangers became a saga of the southwest, but that was much later.

Formerly, Chacon had hung around Galeyville. He ran afoul of Curly Bill and got his scalp laid open by the barrel of Bill's six-gun. As a result, he hated Brocius and all his bunch with a deadly hatred. He had sworn to torture to death any of the Brocius gang that came into his hands. When Lafe Gulden arrived in Pima County, Chacon had already made good his threat in a couple of instances.

Because of the notoriety he quickly achieved, it wasn't difficult for Ringo to get a line on the outlaw; but running him down was another matter. Week after week Ringo stubbornly followed Gulden's trail. Naturally the word got around that he was hunting Gulden. And in the natural sequence of events, Gulden learned of it. It didn't bother Gulden overly much. He felt confident he could keep out of Ringo's way. It was a big country, a hole-in-the-wall country with plenty of hideouts. He was having little trouble dodging sheriffs and marshals. He could dodge Ringo.

But he failed to reckon with Ringo's shrewdness. Ringo plotted the section where Gulden was operating and concentrated on watching what appeared to be likely prospects for a compact and daring outlaw band.

The Tucson-Guamas stage was one. It often carried large shipments of gold and specie. Ringo figured that sooner or later Gulden would make a try for the stage. He took to riding the stage route, keeping out of sight but always with a watchful eye on the clumsy vehicle as it rolled along over canyon trails and between stretches of mesquite that would provide cover for a hundred owlhoots.

So when Gulden and his two companions rode out of the brush that flanked the trail, Ringo was right there waiting for them. A blazing gun battle ensued, in which Gulden's two followers were killed almost before they got into action. Gulden, untouched, whirled his splendid black horse and rode south for the Border. Ringo was blocked by the dead men's horses just long enough to give Gulden a head start. But he felt that his tall roan was as good or better than Gulden's mount. He settled himself in the saddle for a long and gruelling chase. Far ahead, a misty shadow against the skyline, were the mountains of Mexico, where the outlaw might well lose himself if Ringo didn't come up with him before night.

Swiftly the miles rolled back under the roan's flying hoofs and slowly he closed the gap. Ringo began estimating the distance to the Border as against Gulden's lead. He loosened his Winchester in the saddle boot, hesitated, then drew the rifle and tried a couple of shots. Gulden rode on, and Ringo's levelling off the roan's gait for a better shooting stance allowed him to gain a little. He muttered an oath, slid the rifle into its sheath and concentrated on riding. Later he was to regret those fruitless rifle shots.

The sound of gunfire carried a long way in Arizona's clear, dry air. It was plainly heard by a group of dark-faced riders who had paused to water their horses at a little spring bubbling up in a tangle of mesquite at the foot of the long slope down which the black and the roan were speeding.

Unnoticed by either Gulden or Ringo, the group watched the race with interest. Long before Gulden had negotiated the slope the beady-eyed watchers were crouched in the mesquite on either side of the trail, waiting.

Gulden reached the bottom of the slope and flashed along the straight gray track between the mesquite. The hidden watchers let him pass. They could deal safely with but one, and decided it was better to make their try for the pursuer. The pursued wasn't likely to turn back.

When Ringo reached the bottom of the slope, Gulden was still in sight but far ahead. He urged the roan to greater speed.

Something leaped up from the thick dust like a striking snake, tightened with the hum of a sharply smitten harp string. The taut rope caught the speeding roan at the knees. He hurtled over it in a crashing fall. Ringo was catapulted from the saddle. He struck the ground with stunning force, the dust cushioning his fall somewhat. Before he could make a move, lithe, sinewy figures darted from the undergrowth and swarmed all over him. He was jerked to his feet, his arms pinned to his sides by turn on turn of rawhide rope. His guns were plucked from their holsters.

Three hundred yards to the front, Gulden turned in his saddle and gazed back. He slackened his horse's speed.

A shot rang out. Gulden felt the wind of the passing bullet. He glanced back once more at his helpless pursuer, hunched low in the saddle and rode on.

One of his swarthy captors peered into Ringo's face and swore a Spanish oath:

"*Sangre de Cristo!* It is the *Señor* Ringo, the *Señor* Brocius' friend! *Un Gran General* will be pleased to see him, most pleased!"

Ringo went a bit cold. He knew very well whom the half-breed meant. "The Great General," his men called Augustino Chacon. He had been taken by some of Chacon's raiders, and they had recognized him. He was on considerable of a spot.

John Ringo wasn't afraid to die. He'd proved that many times. But there are ways of dying that no man can contemplate with equanimity. Ringo had once seen what was left of a man who had been pegged over an ant hill by just such a bunch. Ants were running into one eyeless socket and out the other. And the man was still alive!

Ringo's horse lay dead, its neck broken by the

fall. His captors lifted him to the back of a shaggy mustang and tied his ankles together by means of a rope drawn under the animal's belly. They spoke among themselves in gutturals that Ringo did not understand. The whole band mounted and rode south. Soon they were across the Border and in Mexico.

Well past mid-afternoon they entered a gloomy canyon. A mile farther on they reached the 'breeds' camp, a half-circle of rude but strongly built huts set in a belt of thicket that hid them from view. Again a cold chill swept over Ringo as he saw, in the center of an open space before the huts, a stout post blackened and charred by eating flames. In the ashes at its base lay a heap of fire-seared chains.

The 'breeds lifted him from his horse and led him to the post. The chains were wrapped around his body and made fast. Twigs and faggots were piled about his feet till the heap was waist high. Then his captors left and entered the huts. Sounds of a meal being prepared were heard. Blind with weariness, his body aching from the effects of the fall he had suffered, Ringo sagged in his bonds, too utterly worn out and miserable to care much what happened to him.

The hours passed slowly. The 'breeds, absorbed in their own activities, did not see the glittering pale eyes that from the concealment of a dense thicket noted their every move.

Just at sunset there was a sound of an approaching horse's hoofs on the stones. A man rode into the clearing, a tall, strikingly handsome man with glowing eyes and a cruelly sinister face. Ringo recognized him instantly.

"Chacon himself!" he muttered. "So he's what they've been waiting for."

Chacon dismounted and strode over to the captive. A slow smile played across his face. His expression was one of terrible gloating.

"*Señor* Ringo!" he exclaimed mockingly. "This is indeed the great pleasure."

Ringo said nothing. He set his jaw and looked the bandit squarely in the eye. He'd be hanged if he'd give Chacon the pleasure of seeing him crawl.

In a thicket the unseen watcher drew a gun and cocked it.

"One slug for Chacon when he orders the fire lit, and one for Ringo," Lafe Gulden breathed to himself. "After that we'll see."

But Chacon did not give the order. He turned to his followers and said in Spanish:

"Get the chains off him. Lock him in the cabin. Give him food. Give him drink. A man must be strong to die well, and slowly. This one is half dead already. By morning he will have recovered."

Ringo was loosed. The ropes that still swathed his numbed arms were cut. Reeling and staggering, he was shoved into one of the end cabins. It had no windows. The door was of stout planks and opened outward. A heavy wooden bar laid in slots secured it on the outside. Built against one wall was a bunk on which were tumbled blankets. He heard the door slam shut, the bar drop into place. He lurched to the bunk and sat down.

After a while some measure of his strength had returned. He got stiffly to his feet and groped about the dark room. There was a chink in the door. He placed his eye to it and saw that a guard with a rifle was stationed just outside. Escape was impossible. He walked back to the bunk. A few minutes later the door opened. A heaping plate of food and a jar of water were shoved in. The door thudded shut again.

Ringo was parched with thirst and drank gratefully of the water. He forced himself to eat of the food, although he had little appetite. He wanted to build up his strength as much as he could. Then when his captors came for him he would put up a desperate fight, hoping to force them to shoot him. After he had cleaned the plate, he threw himself on the bunk and was almost instantly asleep.

Ringo knew he must have been sleeping many hours when he awakened with a start. A faint bar of light was streaming across his face through the open door.

"Ringo!" came a whisper from the darkness.

"Yes?" Ringo whispered back.

"Come out of it," said the unseen speaker. "Don't make a noise."

Ringo swung his feet to the floor and tiptoed across the room to the door. There a figure loomed, a slender, lance-straight figure.

"Gulden!" Ringo breathed. "What the devil?"

"I just don't aim to see those black rascals do to any white man what they figure to do to you, that's all," Gulden replied. "Come on or we're sunk; it's nearly daylight. I thought the sons would never go to sleep. Come on; I got a horse for you. Found him strayin' in the brush. No saddle, rope for a bridle, but a horse."

With Ringo following close behind, Gulden darted for the growth behind the cabin. Just as they reached it, a blood-curdling yell seemed to fill heaven and earth.

"That blasted guard!" Gulden swore. "I didn't hit him hard enough. Come on, feller!"

He crashed through the brush, Ringo at his heels. They reached a little cleared space where stood two horses, Gulden's black and a shaggy mustang.

Gulden flung himself into the saddle. Ringo mounted bareback. The outlaw set the pace and they went crashing through the brush to the more open floor of the canyon. Behind them sounded the shouts and curses of the aroused 'breeds.

"They'll be after us pronto, but we got a start," yelped Gulden. "Ride!"

They rode, the horses floundering over the

rocks but going at a good pace. Gulden slowly drew ahead.

"What's the matter?" he asked, twisting in his saddle. "Can't you keep up?"

"This horse is lame," Ringo answered. "Reckon that's why he was straying loose. He's doing the best he can."

Gulden swore and slowed his mount. They clattered from the canyon mouth and headed north.

"It's going to be touch and go," Gulden said. "I hear 'em. They're coming fast." He drew his rifle from the saddle boot and passed it to Ringo.

"We'll take some of the black rascals along with us, anyhow," he said grimly. "I got my sixes."

Ringo arrived at a sudden decision. Gulden had saved him from a terrible death at the risk of his own life. He deserved a break.

"Ride on," he told Gulden. "You've got a good horse; you can make it. I'll hold 'em back a spell."

"Shut up!" Gulden answered. "Try and get some speed out of that fleabag. We'll see it through together. I'm itching to line sights on some of 'em."

With the mustang limping badly, they rode on. They crashed through a straggle of thicket and reached the semblance of a trail. A few minutes later Ringo twisted in his saddle and sighted his pursuers. They were coming like the wind and were not six hundred yards distant.

"Ten of 'em," Gulden counted. "Big odds, but we'll do what we can. Ride! There's a clump of rocks ahead."

The 'breeds swiftly closed the distance. Lead began whining past. Ringo glanced back again. They were a scant two hundred yards distant. The rocks that might afford some shelter were still nearly a quarter of a mile ahead.

Ringo jerked his laboring mount to a halt and dropped to the ground. He faced the pursuit and clamped the rifle butt to his shoulder. He was totally unprepared for Gulden's move. With a high-pitched screech, like a weasel's battle scream, the outlaw whirled his horse and charged straight at the yelling 'breeds, a blazing gun in each hand.

Two of the 'breeds spun from their saddles. A third fell, and still another.

But the odds were too great. Gulden suddenly rose in his stirrups, reeled sideways and thudded to the ground.

Ringo opened up with the rifle, pouring lead into the demoralized tangle of howling men and plunging horses. With two shots he dropped two of the raiders. A third went down. The others were struck by panic. They whirled their horses and fled madly back the way they had come. Ringo downed still another before they were out of range.

"Seven out of ten; not so bad," he muttered. He dropped the empty rifle and ran to where Gulden lay on his face, his life draining out through his shattered lungs. He turned the outlaw over and raised him in his arms. The mad glitter was gone from the pale eyes. They were clouded with the shadow of Death's hovering wing. Suddenly, however, a flash of intelligence crossed their glazed surface. Gulden's pointed teeth showed white in a weasel grin.

"Ringo, the joke's on you," he whispered through the blood frothing in his throat. "I'm—givin'—you—the—slip!"

His eyes closed, he sighed chokingly, and was dead.

Ringo rose to his feet and gazed down at the motionless form.

"Feller," he said, "you deserve to rest peaceful. Reckon I've got the time, even if those hombres get reorganized and come back, which I don't figure they will."

First he reloaded the rifle, picked up Gulden's fallen Colts and thrust them into his own empty holsters. Then he hunted around till he found a suitable crevice. Into it he gently lowered Gulden's limp body. He jammed the crevice with boulders, heaping them in a low mound above it.

"Reckon that'll keep you safe from the coyotes," he said as he straightened his aching back.

He gazed down at the little mound and eulogized Lafe Gulden with the finest compliment the rangeland can pay:

"Bad all the way through, vicious as a Gila monster, but—a man to ride the river with!"

CHAPTER XIV

Now and then, especially when money was needed for the eternal poker games, John Ringo planned and led an expedition, always successfully. Only a widely read and imaginative man could have conceived the outlandish scheme that cost the Chiricahua Cattle Company, generally called the Cherry Cow, a big herd.

In Galeyville, Ringo lived alone in a small house. When he wasn't playing cards or drinking, he spent most of his time reading. Folks used to say that the only things Ringo ever spent money for were whiskey and books. He was a connoisseur of both.

Aside from drinking and playing cards with them, Ringo never mingled much in a social way with the other outlaws. About the only exception aside from young Billy Clanton, who had been a sort of protégé of Ringo's, was Boone Logan.

Logan was a grizzled old Border fighter and considerable of a character. He had been a soldier in the Civil War and had a few scars to show for it. He was a scout for Lieutenant A. W. Whipple when the latter surveyed the route for Beale's road from Fort Defiance, New

Mexico, to the Colorado River. He helped Beale construct the road, which was later followed by the Sante Fe Railroad line and U.S. Highway 66. Unlike most of his ilk, he was widely travelled, having been on the sea in his youth.

Ringo liked to listen to his yarns, and Logan, who had little education but an avid curiosity about all things, would sometimes laboriously spell out a few passages in a book recommended by Ringo. Mostly, however, he would sit by the window while Ringo read, smoking in silence save for an occasional remark or question.

One afternoon Ringo seemed vastly amused by what he read. He chuckled a good deal, and paused from time to time to stare contemplatively out of the window, his brows drawing together as in thought.

"What's so funny, John?" Logan finally asked.

Ringo laid the book aside and lit his pipe. "I was reading about how Claudius, the Roman Emperor, defeated the Briton chieftain, Caractacus, at the battle of the Weald Brook," he replied to Logan's question. "He did it with camels."

"Camels?"

"That's rght," Ringo said. "Claudius wasn't much of a soldier, but he was a widely read man and a thinker. He just plain outsmarted Caractacus, who was a bang-up general, with camels. Claudius' soldiers made a song about it later."

Chuckling, he picked up the book and read—

" 'Claudius was a famous soldier,
    Claudius shed less blood than ink,
    When he came to fight the Britons
    From the fray he did not shrink,
    But the weapons of his choice were
    Rope and stilts and camel stink.
    Oh, Oh, Oh!' "

"Sounds loco to me," Logan grunted.

"Uh-huh," admitted Ringo, "but it wasn't. You know, Boone, it gives me an idea—an idea how we could get ourselves some nice fat cows. But we'd need a camel or two to do it, and I'm afraid camels aren't easy to come by in Arizona."

Logan looked reflective. "I don't know about that," he said. "I've a notion I might be able to get you a camel."

"Yes?" Ringo was immediately interested.

Logan filled and lighted his pipe. He spat ruminatively out the window, and explained.

"You know, I was with Ed Beale when he built the road from Fort Defiance to the Colorado," he said. "Well, Ed got a notion that camels would be first rate for transport purposes over the desert country. He sold the notion to Jeff Davis, who was Secretary of War. Davis had a couple of shiploads of the critters brought from the Orient. They unloaded 'em at Indianola, Texas, and finally marched 'em overland to Arizona, after holdin' 'em for a while at Camp

Verde. In some ways, Ed Beale's notion was okay. The camels packed big loads, the desert didn't bother 'em a bit, and they were fast; if the going wasn't too rocky they'd leave a horse standing. But they were ugly brutes, ugly as Gila monsters and just as mean. Chaw your arm off if they got a chance, and they never would get friendly like a horse. And horses and mules just couldn't stand 'em. Whenever the horses or mules got around the camels, there was a stampede. And the fellers handed the chore of riding 'em got seasick from their swayin' motion. There was a camel feller came along with 'em on the ship. He could ride 'em, and he tried to teach the other boys how to. But he couldn't stand the mountain climate and threw up his job and went back home. Ed Beale finally give up the whole business. He didn't know what else to do with the critters, so he just turned 'em loose to fend for themselves. Reckon they did, all right. They took to the desert, and there are still quite a few of 'em around over west of the Whetstones."

Logan was right. Some of those camels, or their descendants, were seen on the Arizona deserts as late as 1900.

"So I wouldn't be surprised if I could corral you a camel, if you really want one," Logan concluded. "Where do you figure to get them cows?"

"From the Cherry Cow spread," Ringo answered.

Logan stared at him in astonishment, his jaw dropping. No wonder he thought Ringo had taken leave of his senses. The Cherry Cow Ranch, a big one, was practically impervious to rustling because of its location. It occupied a great bowl surrounded by high steep hills. The trails leading out of the bowl were few, and so steep that cattle could negotiate them only at a panting, shambling walk. The east was the only way open, and that was impractical for rustling purposes. The one trail to the south passed across a shallow river known locally as Horse Creek. The creek could be crossed only by way of the trail, which then flowed steeply upward through a narrow canyon with precipitous walls, where the speed of the herd would be reduced to a crawl.

The Cherry Cow cattle were a challenge to John Ringo, just as the Tombstone Mining and Milling Company's silver bricks had been. He had scouted the terrain a number of times, the south trail across Horse Creek interesting him in particular. Ringo knew that this trail was the logical route by which a stolen herd could reach Mexico and a lucrative market. He rode over it, studied the approach to the canyon via the Horse Creek crossing. One thing he had absently noted: that during the hours between sunset and sunrise, the narrow, shallow gorge through which the creek flowed was always blanketed by a dense mist, due doubtless to the fact that the icy waters of the mountain stream came into contact with the warmer air when the rays of the sun were not present to suck up the fog.

Ringo had been forced reluctantly to give up the notion of tying onto some Cherry Cow beefs. The natural setting being what it was, it just couldn't be done. Then he got his bizarre inspiration from reading about the Emperor Claudius' stratagem at the battle of the Weald Brook.

"Boone," he told Logan, "you get me the camel and I'll get the cows."

"I always figured you'd go plumb loco sooner or later," Logan declared with conviction, adding, "but I guess I am, too. I'll get the camel or die in trying."

So Boone Logan and several of his outlaw companions set out on what was the strangest round-up chore ever attempted by Arizona cowhands—corraling a camel.

They did it, too, after a great deal of riding, much labor and more profanity. They informed Ringo of their success and disposed of the obstinate critter in accordance with his directions. Then Ringo, along with Boone Logan, Pony Deal, Bill Hicks, Frank Patterson and several more of like kidney, descended on the Cherry Cow Ranch with larcenous intentions.

Ringo timed the raid with the utmost nicety. He ascertained that the Cherry Cow had gotten a big trail herd together for immediate shipment. Fat, heavily fleshed cows that would bring

F

top prices. The Cherry Cow owners, having nothing to fear from rustlers, or so they thought, took no precautions to guard the cattle which were held in close herd on a southwest pasture about two miles from the ranchhouse. A single night hawk was assigned to prevent straying. The night was still, moonless, and the guard had little to do. The cows, well fed and content, had risen to take their midnight stretch and had lain down again, grunting and rumbling and chewing their cuds. The night hawk, drowsing in his saddle, rode slowly around and around the herd in an effort to keep awake. He glanced at the great clock in the sky and saw that his relief would show up very shortly and give him a chance to tumble into bed. He quickened the pace of his horse a little and rode along the edge of a belt of growth, the tangled branches of which brushed his shoulder with leafy tips.

From the shadow of the growth an arm shot out, rose and fell. The night hawk spun from his saddle to lie huddled on the ground, his scalp split by the slashing blow of a six-gun barrel.

"Shall I stick a knife between his ribs and take him proper?" whispered Pony Deal.

"No, let him wake up after a while and nurse his headache," said Ringo. "His relief will be around in less than an hour, anyhow. Doesn't matter if he comes to a bit early. Get those cows moving, and without any noise. We need a mite of a start."

The expert punchers got the herd moving without difficulty. The sleepy cows protested somewhat but ambled along with little urging. The herd made good time to the mist-swathed banks of Horse Creek and the canyon trail.

The pistol-whipped night guard got his senses back rather sooner than Ringo expected. The blow had been a glancing one and the wound in his head looked worse than it actually was. Once he regained consciousness and noted that his bovine charges were nowhere in sight, it didn't take him long to figure what had happened. Cursing and groaning, he mounted his horse and streaked for the ranchhouse. Ten minutes after his arrival, the Cherry Cow hands, in a very bad temper and led by a salty old range boss, took up the trail. Knowing well that there was but one route out of the valley the rustlers could use, they hightailed for the Horse Creek crossing.

"Those hombres, whoever they are, must be plumb fools," declared the range boss. "If they had the brains of a terrapin they'd know they can't get away with it. We'll catch 'em on the canyon trail and give them a lesson they won't forget soon; that is if there's any left alive to remember. Sift sand! I'm itchin' to line sights with the hellions."

Meanwhile Ringo and his companions had shoved the herd across Horse Creek. The mist in the gorge was so dense they were forced fairly to grope their way. Something seemed to bother the horses, too. They peered and snorted, pricking their ears and glancing nervously upstream. They were reluctant to take the water and required urging. The cattle, however, entered the creek without protest. Ringo allowed them to drink a little of the icy water.

"We're in no particular hurry," he told his companions, "and they've got a hard drive ahead of them. They'll do it better if they fill up a bit here. Okay, shove 'em along up the trail. We'll catch up with you pronto."

The herd moved on, breasting the steep rise, slowing to a slow trudge. Ringo, Patterson, and Boone Logan halted their horses a hundred yards or so above the south bank of the creek. They dismounted and tethered the animals securely.

"Not taking any chances with them," observed Ringo. "They might get a whiff. I don't care to walk from here to Mexico."

He and the others waded the shallow creek to the north bank. They groped their way upstream for some distance and gingerly approached a dense thicket. There followed a period of singular activity accompanied by strange sounds and considerable profanity. Then they waded back to the south bank, retrieved their horses and rode to catch up with the laboring herd.

"I hope that trick works, John," Logan remarked nervously. "If it don't, we're gone goslin's. The Cherry Cow crew will be on the trail by now. They'll catch us in the canyon and swoop down on us like forty hen-hawks on a settin' quail. No getting away, with the cows bunched in front of us and those straight-up-and-down cliffs on either side."

"It'll work," Ringo replied in a composed voice. "Don't you worry; it'll work."

The Cherry Cow outfit did not spare their horses. They made fast time to the creek, and everything went smoothly till they raced down the slope to the gorge bottom. Then a contretemps ensued. The horses skated to a halt and absolutely refused to enter the blanket of mist. They snorted, squealed, reared, bucked, and became utterly unmanageable.

The range boss raved, the cowboys cursed, but the horses paid them no heed. They were not going to enter that pall of ghostly white and that was all there was to it. Their nervousness communicated itself to the riders. Apprehensive glances were cast at the motionless fog bank. Only the soft, smothered ripple of the stream was to be heard. Otherwise the night was deathly still, ominously so, as if all nature had been frighted to silence by some lurking horror. Without any order to do so, the cowboys retired to the slope a way to discuss the mystery. The horses quieted somewhat, but they still snorted and shivered and rolled their eyes.

"Something funny about this," declared the

range boss. "You'd think there was a whole herd of mountain lions holed up in that fog, the way the fool cayuses are acting. I——"

From where the mist lay like billows of cotton-wool came a sound, a horrible bubbling groan, as if a man were trying to cry out with his throat choked with blood.

"What the devil?" yelped a cowboy. "That—Lord almighty!"

From the fog bank bulged a frightful object—a humped, misshapen body, great splay hoofs, long snaky neck, bulging eyes and champing teeth. It groaned and glared and bubbled.

With yells of terror the cowboys whirled their frantic mounts and rode madly away from the apparition. The horses were only too glad to go.

"It's the devil!" a hand howled.

"Pull up!" bellowed the range boss. "Pull up, you fools! It's only a camel."

"Camel, nothin'!" a young puncher from the north shouted back. "There ain't no camels in America! It's Old Nick himself, that's what it is—hoofs, horns, tail, fire and brimstone and all the rest! I wouldn't go back there for all the silver in Tombstone!"

The others were fully in accord with his sentiments. They were a mile distant from the fog-shrouded creek and its grisly horror before they pulled rein.

In vain the range boss explained and argued. The superstitious cowboys couldn't see it his way.

They preferred to stay right where they were.
Finally one voiced a clincher.

"What's the sense in goin' back, anyhow?"
he asked. "We can't get the horses into that
infernal fog."

"Guess you're right about that," the range
boss was forced to admit. It's tainted with the
smell of that humped-back hellion, and a horse
can't stand the smell of a camel."

"I've noticed they don't like the smell of
sulphur, either," the cowboy from the north
remarked significantly. The range boss swore at
him and made little impression.

The hands wanted to go home, but the range
boss persuaded them to stay until daybreak.
After the sun had sucked up the mist, he rode
back to the creek. He rode alone, his men
declining to accompany him.

As he expected, he found the scoring of great
splay hoofs in the soft earth of the creek bank,
where Ringo had marched the camel back and
forth. The animal itself had disappeared and
was never seen again. Doubtless it made its way
back to the desert, not knowing that it was
destined to become a legend.

Meanwhile the stolen herd was well on its
way to Mexico and a lucrative market.

"I've a notion the Weald Brook was the same
sort of a stream as Horse Creek," Ringo ex-
explained to Logan as they trotted along beside
the fast-moving herd. "Anyhow, it was blanketed

with a clammy mist at night. Claudius ran his camels up and down through the mist till it was rank with the smell of them, and when Caractacus' chariots charged, the horses stopped at the mist and threw his whole van into confusion. Claudius used ropes stretched knee-high between tent stakes in the tall grass to make the mixup worse, but I figured a camel would do the trick for us. Looks like it did."

"It sure does," chuckled Logan. "It was a mighty smart trick. John, if you'd just ridden a straight trail instead of gotten mixed up with gamblers and rustlers, I figure you would have ended up a big man. You got all the earmarks. John, why did you do it?"

"Boone," Ringo returned sadly, "I'll be hanged if I know."

The tale was told and retold with gusto and much hilarity in Galeyville, Charleston, and Paradise, but no one was ever able to convince the Cherry Cow punchers that it hadn't been the devil who had charged them from out the Horse Creek fog.

CHAPTER XV

The last flare of the dying lamp! That was John Ringo's raid on an S.P. passenger train. Doubtless, as in other instances, it pleased his sardonic sense of humor to do the apparently impossible.

The local from Tucson often carried large shipments of specie for Benson, from where it would be transferred to Tombstone via a heavily guarded stage. Ringo and the Galeyville bunch had had an eye on those shipments for some time. The problem was how to get one.

"We might dynamite the train and then shoot it out with the express messenger," suggested impetuous Billy Claibourne as they discussed the matter one night.

Ringo shook his head decisively. "No good," he said. "There would be women riding that train, and maybe kids. Can't take a chance on hurting them."

Knowing Ringo's attitude toward women and children, the others did not press the point.

"Besides," said Ringo, "shooting it out with the messenger might prove to be considerable of a chore. The advantage would all be on his side—fighting behind locked doors and with us out in the open. And no telling who might be riding that train. We might find we'd worried off a bit more than we could chaw. Let it ride for a while. I'll do a bit of scouting and thinking. If the job is to be pulled, it will have to be pulled smoothly and in a way to catch everybody off guard. I'll think about it a bit."

The rest of the bunch, who had confidence in Ringo as a thinker, nodded agreement.

Ringo took to riding the railroad right-of-way from Tucson to Benson until he was thoroughly familiar with the fifty-odd miles of rough and lonely country. He noted a few things that interested him. One was that there was a flag stop six or seven miles east of Tucson, where the train often paused to unload small shipments of machinery or other items for the mines back in the hills; also at times to pick up a shipment of equipment being sent east for repairs. He noted that such shipments were always delivered by wagon crews who handled the loading. The express agent would look over the bills of lading and sign for the shipment, otherwise paying it little mind.

Those ponderous crates and packing cases interested Ringo. One day while he was watching a shipment being loaded, he chuckled. John Ringo had abruptly gotten an idea, the nebulous outlines of a plan as bizarre as the one that had cost the Cherry Cow Ranch a valuable herd.

Perhaps he really got the idea from reading Homer. It bore some resemblance to the stratagem of the Trojan Horse.

His followers were somewhat dubious when he outlined the plan. It was just a bit daring even for those hardened campaigners.

"Good gosh! if something should slip!" sputtered Claibourne. "We'd all be roped and hogtied for delivery to the calaboose."

"No reason for anything to slip," replied Ringo. "As I see it, it's a natural. I'm willing to take the chance if you boys are."

"Okay," agreed Claibourne. "It's so loco it might work. I'm with you, John."

The others nodded agreement.

One evening about ten days later, just as dusk was falling, the east-bound local was flagged down. Next to the engine was the express car, presided over by a watchful messenger with a Colt strapped to his waist. A heavy wagon loaded with four long packing cases set on end and roped in place pulled up alongside the car. Four burly individuals descended from the wagon and shouted for the messenger. One carried a sheaf of bills of lading.

"Machinery headed east for repairs," he told the messenger when the door of the express car was opened. "Here are the bills. Look 'em over, feller, and see if everything is okay. Here's the book for you to sign."

The messenger glanced at the bills. "Okay,"

he said. "Load it up, and shake a leg; we're late already."

The speaker for the wagoneers thrust the signed book in his pocket.

"All right, boys," he told his companions. "Handle that stuff carefully. Some of it is delicate. Bust it up worse than it is and somebody'll be sent a hefty bill of damages and we'll be in hot water. Easy, now."

The cases were carried into the car with great care and stood on end along one side wall. The boss of the wagoneers roped them securely in place.

"Can't take a chance on 'em toppling over when you scoot around a curve," he told the watchful messenger, who stood with one hand on his gun butt. "Okay, I reckon that ought to do it. Let's go, boys."

They piled out of the car. The messenger waved a highball to the engineer, slid the door shut and double-locked it. As the train got under way he sat down at his desk and busied himself with paper work, now and then glancing instinctively at the tall iron safe standing in one end of the car.

The train roared on through the night. A full moon soared up over the eastern hills, and light like molten silver flowed over the silent wasteland. Details stood out hard and clear, and the shadows of the mesquite thickets were as black and solid-looking as the trees themselves. The steel rails shimmered in the headlight's beam as the great drivers hammered the high iron to the accompaniment of clanging side-rods and thundering exhaust. The train was late and making up time.

The messenger was still bent over his desk, absorbed in his work. Suddenly he raised his head, his attention attracted by a creaking sound behind him. He half turned in his chair, clutched spasmodically at his gun, then "froze," his jaw sagging, his eyes bulging. The front of one of the packing cases had slid open like a door. Stepping from the case was a tall, broad-shouldered man wearing a black mask and holding a cocked gun that was trained on the messenger's back. Through the holes cut in the mask his eyes gleamed coldly.

"Okay, boys," he shouted above the roar of the train. "Come on out."

The fronts of the other cases slid back, and from each stepped a masked and armed man.

The tall leader approached the paralyzed messenger. He plucked the big Colt from its sheath and shoved it under his belt. With his gun barrel he gestured to the safe in the end of the car.

"All right," he said, "open that box before I open your head with this gun barrel."

The messenger hesitated; but a glance at the icy eyes glaring at him through the mask holes convinced him that resistance would be not only futile but doubtless fatal. He moved to the safe, the gun muzzle against his back, and went to work on the combination knob with trembling fingers. A few twirls and the tumblers clicked. He turned the door handle, the bolts shot back and the door swung open. The inner door responded to the manipulation of a key.

John Ringo, his gun ready for instant action, shoved him aside. His followers began tumbling plump canvas sacks onto the floor. When the safe was empty they gathered them up, grunting under their weight.

The messenger was securely lashed to his chair. Ringo stood peering out the window. He gave a grunt of satisfaction a moment later as he spotted a stone outcropping on a tall ridge.

"Right ahead is the grove where Pete will be waiting with the horses," he observed. He reached up and grasped the emergency cord. With a slow, steady pull he opened the valve. Air gushed through the ports, and there was a grinding of brake shoes on the wheels. The locomotive exhaust was abruptly shut off as the engineer slammed his throttle shut at the screech of the brakes. The train jolted to a stop.

"Get going and load the stuff," Ringo told the others. "Pete's coming out with the horses. Come on, Bill; head for the engine."

The engineer and fireman were both leaning out the window, peering back along the train. The next instant they were looking into Ringo's gun muzzle.

"Down out of it," he told them. "Move!"

The bewildered trainmen obeyed. A light bobbed from the rear coach. The conductor was hurrying over to see what was wrong. A couple of bullets whined past him and sent him hunting cover. While Billy Claibourne held his gun on the enginemen, Ringo mounted to the locomotive cab.

Ringo knew considerable about locomotives. He jerked the mud valve open and sent steam and hot water bellowing from the boiler. Not until the steam gauge needle showed but a few pounds pressure did he close the valve and descend from the cab.

"All right," he told the enginemen. "Reckon it'll take a while for you to get up enough steam to move her. Enough time for us to get in the clear before you reach Benson. So long!"

He and Claibourne mounted their waiting horses. The tight group rode north at full speed.

In the engine cab of the stalled locomotive was intense activity. The fireman, the blower wide open, was shovelling coal into the firebox.

"The darn fool didn't realize that, with the water at this low level, it would take only a jiffy to get up enough steam to get going!" he chuckled to the engineer. "And the Ellis water tank ain't but a couple miles farther on. Loading pens there, and a telegraph operator. We'll stop and send a wire. Those gun-slingin' gents will find themselves trying to outrun a posse."

The conductor, reassured by the outlaws'

departure, clambered into the cab. A brakeman had already released the express messenger, who was interspersing his story of what happened with appalling profanity.

"Get her moving quick as you can, Ad," the conductor told the engineer. "I'll have a wire ready to send when we reach Ellis. The robbers didn't figure on that."

But that was just what Ringo *had* figured on. He knew it would take only a few minutes to get the train under way. But a few minutes were all he needed. Once out of sight behind the growth, he and Claibourne turned their horses and rode east, parallelling the right-of-way. And Claibourne had a pair of wire cutters in his pocket. Before the headlight of the locomotive stabbed around the curve, Ringo and Claibourne were holed up behind the little shack occupied by the telegraph operator.

The train ground to a stop. The conductor dropped down the steps and ran to the shack, shouting and waving a paper.

"Send it fast!" he told the operator, and ran back to the train, waving a highball with his lantern.

The operator was just opening his key when the masked Ringo stepped into the room, gun in hand.

"Close that key!" he ordered.

The operator didn't like the look of that cocked Colt. He obeyed orders without arguing.

"The message the con gave you," Ringo said, "let's have it."

He took the paper from the trembling operator and glanced at it.

"Okay," he said. "You can send it now. Only where it says, 'They headed north,' make it read, 'They headed south.' And don't try any tricks if you want to stay healthy. I understand Morse pretty well."

The operator opened his key with a shaking hand; the sender began to chatter. Ringo stood behind him, listening attentively.

Possibly Ringo could not really follow the code of dots and dashes; but with that gun muzzle pressing between his shoulder blades, the operator took no chances. He followed instructions to the letter. When he had gotten his repeat and closed the key, Ringo sat down in a chair and rolled a cigarette with his left hand. He passed it to the operator and rolled one for himself.

"Reckon you've got a gun in that drawer," he remarked, blowing out a cloud of smoke from under his mask. "Well, guess you'd better leave it there."

"Take it if you want it," quavered the operator.

"Don't reckon I need to," Ringo replied. "Keep it—guns cost money."

A few minutes later, Claibourne thrust his masked face in the door. "Okay," he said. "Everything taken care of."

Ringo stood up, nodded to the operator and walked out.

As soon as he heard the click of departing hoofbeats, the operator grabbed his key and opened it. Nothing happened. The young and athletic Claibourne, climbing the telegraph pole with wire cutters in his pocket, had taken care of that.

At Benson, a posse was gotten together in hot haste.

"The scoundrels are headed for the Huachuca Mountains," was the general agreement. "We'll be riding the short diagonal. We'll get 'em!"

Before the train pulled in, the posse had departed on a long, tiresome and fruitless ride.

Meanwhile, Ringo and his companions, having skirted Benson, were jogging along east by a bit south at a leisurely pace. They had a clear trail to the Chiricahuas and Galeyville.

The proceeds of the robbery were spent on cars, women and whisky, and general hilarity in which Ringo took little part. He was morose and depressed and wanted no man's company.

The lamp was burning low.

CHAPTER XVI

Tombstone had sprung into being on its cactus flats almost overnight, which was not uncommon for towns where unexpected strikes of metal had been made; but the fall of Tombstone is unique in mining annals.

All over the West are to be seen rotting ruins and grass-grown streets where once were flourishing settlements. The springs of their wealth gradually dried up, the mines closed down and they were abandoned. Others achieved permanency, their citizens turning to other pursuits; but seldom did they regain their pristine splendor. Virginia City roared and thundered in the shadow of Mount Davidson. The great Comstock Lode slowly petered out and Virginia City sank into obscurity. Hangtown was once a serious contender of San Francisco and Sacramento in wealth and population; such financial giants as Mark Hopkins, Philip D. Armour and John Studebaker started their careers there. But the returns from placer mines in the ravines dwindled, and today, bereft of even its former picturesque name, Placerville, California, is a modest village in a fruit-growing section. The fates of Gold Hill, El Dorado, and many others were similar.

However, their decline was gradual, in some instances covering a period of years. They grew up like mushrooms and finally succumbed to slow decay.

Tombstone was different. At high noon the clock struck midnight, and from the metropolis of the southwest, Tombstone became a quiet hamlet servicing the ranches of the neighboring valleys. There was no slow decay for Tombstone. She was more like a crushed puffball exploding in a cloud of smoke.

Nor did the springs of Tombstone's wealth dry up—quite the contrary. The Tombstone silver is still there under the naked, sun-blasted hills. And it's there to stay!

At the 500-foot level of the Sulphuret Mine a gang of rock busters were slogging at the cracked and seamed head of a drift. Drills chattered, sledges thudded, picks tumbled slabs of rock. Water streamed down the face of the drift, retarding progress, bringing great discomfort to the workers. Mud clogged the drills. The sledge handles were slippery. The laborers sloshed and floundered and cursed the day they were born.

"It's one of those blasted springs," swore the exasperated drift foreman. "We might as well put in a few charges and blow down the face. A pool must have backed up in there. We'll let it out and drain it off. Get the drills and other stuff back out of the way. Powder men on the job!"

The charges were rammed home with difficulty because of the intruding water. The dynamite was capped, the fuses cut along. The workers retired some distance along the gallery, lit their pipes and sat down to rest and smoke. Finally the long-drawn yell of "Pow-w-wder!" echoed along the passage. The cap lights of the powder men bobbed through the darkness. They threw themselves down beside the others and waited.

A few minutes passed, and the hollow boom of the explosion made the air quiver, followed by the thudding and crackling of falling rock. The foreman arose and stretched. Time to go back and clean up the mess. But the rumbling and thudding did not cease; it grew in volume, changed to a mighty roar.

"What in blazes?" sputtered the bewildered foreman. "Did we bring the whole roof down with that blow?"

He peered along the gallery. The cap lights penetrated the gloom for but a few yards. Suddenly he saw a pale vision rushing toward them to the accompaniment of horrific sound.

"Run!" he yelled. "Get in the clear! We've tapped the whole blasted Pacific Ocean!"

The terrified workers raced along the gallery at top speed, the flood roaring at their very heels. They reached a side gallery that sloped steeply upward and darted into it. Behind them the black water raved and thundered. Fright lent wings to their feet, and on the steep slope of the gallery they were able to do a little better than hold their own. But when, panting and exhausted, they reached the shaft and the waiting cage that would whisk them upward to safety, the water was roaring into the sump and sloshing about their knees. They piled into the cage and were drawn upward to the outer air.

On the surface the pumps were clanking furiously. Muddy streams poured from the overflow pipes, but the water rose and rose. Workers were streaming from the mine as gallery after gallery was flooded. The irritation and disgust of the mine officials changed to disquietude, then became genuine alarm. Reports were pouring in from the other pits. The water was seeping into their galleries also. Geysers as thick as a man's body spouted from the floors of the tunnels. The disaster was widespread. The Lucky Cuss, the Tough Nut, the East and West, the Goodenough, the Contention—all reported trouble.

The pumps could not handle the flood. More and better pumps were telegraphed for and were rushed to the scene. As soon as they were installed, men said, the water would be drained off and work resumed. It was but a temporary setback, nothing really to worry about. Tombstone believed what was said and went its merry, turbulent way. Everywhere was gayety and laughter and ebullient optimism. Even better times were in the making. The hundreds of miners went about enjoying their enforced vacation. Only in the mine offices did worried engineers discuss the matter gravely with even more worried owners. What was said behind these closed doors was kept a tight secret. No sense in scaring people. Everything would work out in the end.

Ringo and Johnny Behan were drinking together in the Crystal Palace saloon. The little sheriff was voluble and optimistic. "It don't mean a thing," he reiterated over and over. "Soon as they get that new machinery installed they'll pump out the mines and get going again. Times will be better than they ever were. It don't mean a thing."

"Johnny," Ringo replied, "you're talking through your hat, and I've a feeling you know that you are. There's no use trying to fool yourself. This town is done for. There'll never be another ounce come out of those mines. The silver of the Tombstone Hills might as well be encased in a million feet of steel for all the good it'll ever do anybody. They've tapped a great subterranean lake or river. The water will keep coming, no matter now much pumping they do. If they installed a pump on every square yard of surface, they couldn't stop the flow. Might as well face it. Tombstone is already dead. Just a corpse walking around. It'll soon tumble over."

"I think you're wrong, John," the sheriff protested. But the words sounded hollow in his own ears.

About midnight Ringo left the saloon. Like a somber shadow he passed through the swirling crowds. The feverish activity around him seemed to him like the jerky movements of a corpse. Tombstone was dead. Soon the roaring boom town would sink to the status of a lonely hamlet in the hills. He walked aimlessly along Fremont Street. Near the gloom of the O.K. corral, where men had died in blood, he paused, gazing at the sky.

Over the Dragoons the moon hung red. Ringo knew that those coned and rounded mountains had once been volcanoes, spouting fire and smoke, flaming with thundering life. Now they were cold and silent. For how many untold ages, he wondered, had the dead orb above and the dead hills below gazed upon each other, and in the utter solitude of space poured forth each to each the tale of their lost life and long-departed glory, and told each other stories of the days of earth's youngness and the wonders thereof? He recalled a passage from one of his favorite books:—

"Nothing may endure. That is the inexorable law. Men and women, empires and cities, thrones, principalities and powers, mountains, rivers and unfathomable seas, worlds, spaces, and universes, all have their day, and all must go. Nothing can loiter on the road and check the progress of things upward toward Life, or the rush of things downward toward Death."

The glare of Tombstone's lights outshone the stars, but over the Dragoons the baleful moon hung red. Ringo turned and walked back to the roar and bustle of Allen Street.

Ringo's prediction was correct. The costly pumping machinery installed by the Grand Central and Contention mines proved inadequate to the task. The other mine owners, seeing the handwriting on the wall, refused to throw good money after bad. The Grand Central and Contention were trying to drain the whole district, and failing signally. The water rose to a great depth in the shafts all over the hill.

The exodus began. The army of miners departed to other fields. With them departed the prosperity of Tombstone. The Crystal Palace closed. So did the Oriental Bar and other ornate establishments. The Bird Cage Opera House became but a shadow of its former flamboyant self. No longer did famed performers tread its boards. Soon it would become, of all things, a prosaic dining room and a museum of early Tombstone history.

Ore wagons no longer rumbled along Allen Street, nor did the great wains loaded with lumber from the sawmills in the Chiricahuas and Huachucas. The clattering hoofs of a lonely cowboy's pony sounded loud in the subdued murmur that had once been a bellowing roar. No silver bricks flattened the springs of the groaning stagecoach. The Contention and Charleston mills closed down. Their horde of workers vanished. The plate-glass windows that had been squares and rectangles of ruddy gold were opaquely staring eyes, with only clustering shadows where mirth and revelry had once held sway. Charleston, Contention, and Paradise were ghost towns, and Tombstone was well on the way to joining them.

CHAPTER XVII

John Ringo rode slowly along almost deserted Allen Street. On either side were the opaque eyes of empty windows, the blank finality of locked doors. A ghostly hush hung over the street. The gurgle of water in a gutter was like the rattling breath in the throat of a dying man. Here and there a depressed shop owner lounged under a wooden awning and stared moodily at nothing. The mahogany bars that had gleamed like polished mirrors in the lamplight were sifted with a film of dust. The crystal pendants of the chandeliers hung listlessly, devoid of glints and sparkles.

A few citizens trudged along in the dispirited fashion of men who have nothing to do and no particular destination in mind. A rooster wallowed in a heap of dust, essayed a futile crow that broke off in the middle of a note. A dog scratched industriously, pricked his ears at the passing horseman but apparently lacked the ambition to bark. Above the town the openings of the mine shafts gaped like yawning mouths. There was no rumble of machinery, no hum of busy workers. In a cheap saloon a bartender in a dirty apron served drinks in unwashed glasses.

A listless poker game for very small stakes was in progress at a table devoid of cloth. The sky was gray and there was a clammy chill in the air.

Ringo had been drinking all day, but he was far from drunk. A great cloud of depression had descended upon him, and the alcohol he had consumed had little effect. Now he rode aimlessly out of town, his head bowed, his eyes brooding. He reached the outskirts of the town and glanced back upon the desolation that a short time before had been a scene of booming activity. The melancholy scene reflected his own mood of profound dejection. The flame that had burned so brightly was no more; only the smoking wick remained.

As he rode, Ringo's hopeless despondency deepened. He rode aimlessly, apparently not caring where he went. He paused at Antelope Springs and drank all evening in Jack McCann's saloon. He was in the saddle again the next morning, gloomier than the night before. His next stop was Soldier Holes. He was so moody, his eyes so tortured, that people instinctively avoided him.

Ringo did not appear to notice. He drank alone, taciturn, aloof, speaking to no one, not even the bartenders. A slight motion of his hand, tipping his empty glass, made known his wants. When he left Soldier Holes late in the afternoon, his tall form was erect, his shoulders squared, his step sure. Only the terrible look in his eyes warned the observant that he was approaching the cold, dank realm of utter madness.

As dusk was falling he made his last stop, Myers Cinega in Sulphur Springs Valley. In the Widow Patterson's drinking spot he met Billy Claibourne and Buckskin Frank Leslie. They had been on a ten-day spree together and greeted Ringo with drunken enthusiasm.

In the company of these boon companions, Ringo seemed to perk up a little. He talked and drank with them, and not until after midnight did he again sink into the depths of black despair. Finally he went to bed and fell into a sodden sleep, awakening the following afternoon. Leslie and Claibourne were still sleeping. Ringo did not awaken them. After a couple of drinks and no breakfast, he rode away.

Where Turkey Creek Canyon opened out into Sulphur Springs Valley, Ringo drew rein. He dismounted and seated himself on a boulder. Above the western crags the sun was sinking in blood. It was just such a sunset as the one that had welcomed Ringo when he had ridden into Galeyville to meet with Curly Bill Brocius.

For a long time he sat motionless, staring into the red glare of the sun. Scenes of long ago, long forgotten, stole through his mind and caused him to smile faintly. His dejection vanished. Gradually his lined and haggard face seemed to grow smooth and youthful. The tormented look in his eyes was supplanted by an expression of great peace. He smiled more widely as he gazed on the beauty of the summer landscape.

The long tally of the lonely years was ended. Still smiling, he drew one of his ivory-handled Colts from its holster. He drew back the hammer to full cock. With a steady hand he raised the gun till the cold steel circle of the muzzle pressed against his temple.

The smile remained on his lips.

Leslie Scott was born in Lewisburg, West Virginia. During the Great War, he joined the French Foreign Legion and spent four years in the trenches. In the 1920s he worked as a mining engineer and bridge builder in the western American states and in China before settling in New York. A bar-room discussion in 1934 with Leo Margulies, who was managing editor for Standard Magazines, prompted Scott to try writing fiction. He went on to create two of the most notable series characters in Western pulp magazines. In 1936, Standard Magazines launched, and in *Texas Rangers*, Scott under the house name of **Jackson Cole** created Jim Hatfield, Texas Ranger, a character whose popularity was so great with readers that this magazine featuring his adventures lasted until 1958. When others eventually began contributing Jim Hatfield stories, Scott created another Texas Ranger hero, Walt Slade, better known as *El Halcon*, the Hawk, whose exploits were regularly featured in *Thrilling Western*. In the 1950s Scott moved quickly into writing book-length adventures about both Jim Hatfield and Walt Slade in long series of original paperback Westerns. At the same time, however, Scott was also doing some of his best work in hardcover Westerns published by Arcadia House; thoughtful, well-constructed stories, with engaging characters and authentic settings and situations. Among the best of these, surely, are *Silver City* (1953), *Longhorn Empire* (1954), *The Trail Builders* (1956), and *Blood on the Rio Grande* (1959). In these hardcover Westerns, many of which have never been reprinted, Scott proved himself highly capable of writing traditional Western stories with characters who have sufficient depth to change in the course of the narrative and with a degree of authenticity and historical accuracy absent from many of his series stories.